# PRIMEVAL
# RANCH

A DINO RIFT SPIN-OFF

# PRIMEVAL RANCH

## DEREK BORNE
## & A.L. BORNE

# PRIMEVAL RANCH

Edited by R.A. Milhoan Book Services
Cover Design and Interior Formatting by We Got You Covered Book Design
WWW.WEGOTYOUCOVEREDBOOKDESIGN.COM
Photograph of Derek Borne by Tara Jeles – So Jeles Photography
Creature Sketches by Devon Kahles

This is a work of fiction. All characters, names, places, organizations and events portrayed in this novel are a product of the author's imagination. Any resemblance to persons, living or dead, actual events, or organizations is entirely coincidental.

No dinosaurs or prehistoric creatures were harmed in the making of this book.

Published by Virtuoso Press

## TO DAD,

*You've given so much of yourself*
*and sacrificed so much for those you love.*
*I'm happy I inherited your passion,*
*and your ability to care so much that it hurts.*
*You're special, and you're enough.*
*There's no other dad I'd rather have.*

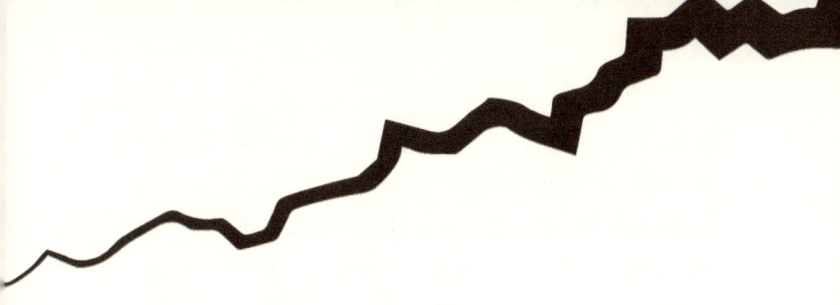

# ONE

## TWO YEARS AGO

**"WAIT, WHAT'S** happening in San Francisco?" a teen boy asked his dad as he claimed his usual spot on the couch.

Having received a text message during dinner, the dad had left his family to see for himself. "Something… indescribable."

"As you can see behind me…*oh my God*…some electrical anomaly has opened up, and vehicles—we don't know how many—have crashed into this forest that's come out of nowhere." The reporter shook her head as she spoke into the news camera. "And some have reported spotting what looks like…*dinosaurs* on the other side."

By now, the Sanchez family had their collective gaze glued to the TV screen.

Family and friends had sent them messages during dinner about the happenings in San Francisco. Leaving their half-eaten *tortas ahogada* on the dining room table, they sat in complete astonishment.

"Are you sure this isn't some kind of movie?" Zavier sent texts back to his high school buddies. "Raymon says it looks like movie CGI."

Humberto leaned closer to the television. "*¡Ay, caray!* this is real, we're living a historical moment right now."

Hand to her chest, Hana sat beside her husband in disbelief. "Why is Lucero not home yet?" She focused on the front door, anxious for her daughter to return from a friend's house.

During the live newsfeed, a deafening roar caused everyone in the affected area to stare at the ominous arc of rift energy.

Hairs stood up on Hana's arms. "*Luz,* where *are* you?"

*CRRRRACK-ACK-ACK! ZAP! CRACKLE! SNAP!*

Lucero pounded the pedals of her bike like her life depended on it.

To her left, a circular opening fringed with bright blue snaps of electricity materialized.

She glanced over while booking it down the trail. "What the *heck?*"

Dinosaurs roared and bellowed from the other side.

Her legs threatened to freeze up, but she pushed on.

*Is this it?* Luz shook her head as she sped up. *Is the world ending?*

Making a turn, she heard a hefty creature galloping from behind.

She managed a quick look over her shoulder.

Something resembling a triceratops thundered after her. Its head frill wore a menacing number of spikes, with one sizeable horn above its snout.

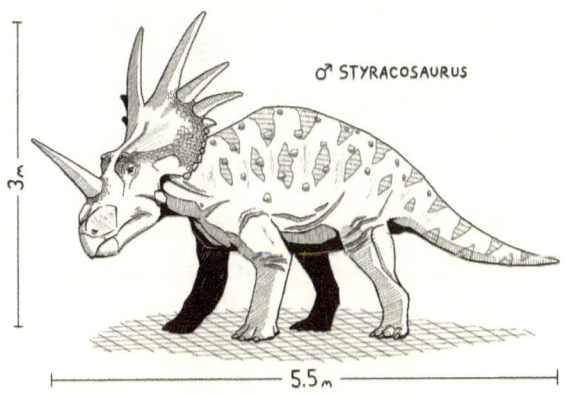

♂ STYRACOSAURUS

3ᵐ

5.5ᵐ

Adrenaline like she'd never experienced before pulsated through her entire body.

"Oh God!" She fought off the burning sensation in her legs. "Come on, I'm too young to—"

*CRRRRACK-ACK-ACK! ZAP! CRACKLE! SNAP!*

Another time rift exploded open.

Luz had no time to react, riding her bike right through it.

Skidding to a stop and resting her trembling legs, she whipped her head around at the dense, otherworldly jungle.

*HRAAAAAAH!*

Her long, dark ponytail swung as she remembered the dinosaur.

It hadn't stopped charging.

Pushing past the agony in her muscles, Luz gave it her all.

While focusing on the rocks and tree roots ahead of her, she heard other humans yelling and honed in on a commotion off to the right.

*BLAM! BLAM! BLAM!*

*ROOOOOOAAAAAARRRR!*

Glancing in the direction of the disturbance, she discovered men with firearms shooting at a pair of large dinosaurs protecting their young. Off to the side of the semi-open area, a pair of teenagers shared a loving embrace.

"Who the heck is all—whoa!" Luz swerved around a cycad plant. "Dinosaurs." Pedaling over a hefty ground vine like a ramp, she finally realized how much old growth surrounded her. "Dinosaurs…*with people?*"

Biking around a rather large ginkgo tree, she made multiple glances back to the group, hoping she wouldn't be spotted.

A crocodilian-like dinosaur leapt onto a man, closing its toothed jaws around his head.

Luz turned her head away, wanting to squeeze her eyelids shut. "Holy—"

*CRRRRACK-ACK-ACK! ZAP! CRACKLE! SNAP!*

Another time rift materialized mere feet away from her.

Hoping it would take her back home, she didn't stop.

As soon as Luz crossed its threshold, she sighed with relief when a farmhouse and weathered wooden fence came into view.

*Z-Z-ZAP! ZZZZEEEEUUUU-POP!*

The blueish window to another time closed inward on

itself.

Huffing and puffing, Luz slowed down and turned her bike to rest. Removing her dominant and exhausted right leg to stand, it gave out beneath her. Tumbling to the dirt road, she landed on her side. Thankfully, she didn't have to worry about being chased anymore.

Every vein and artery in her body slowed their pace as the adrenaline wore off.

Staring up at the star-filled sky, she analyzed the last couple of minutes in her mind.

*Crazy anomaly…check. Insane jungle…check. Dinosaurs… check.* It all added up to one conclusion. *Did I just time travel in and out of prehistoric times?*

Once Luz had regained her strength, she picked her bike back up and hopped on. A thrust with her left foot failed to send her forward. "What? Seriously?" Getting off again, she checked on the chain of her hand-me-down bike. "Broken." She rolled her eyes and sighed in frustration. "Well, this is freaking excellent."

Figuring she'd ended up out in the country, she didn't recognize the road or scenery. Looking over at the farmhouse once more, she noted a light from within. Picking up her busted bike, she trudged forward. "This better be my time."

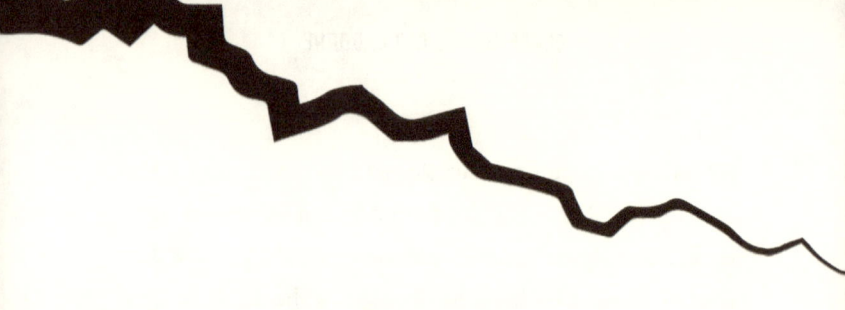

# TWO

### SAME YEAR ... FIVE MINUTES AGO

**BOISTEROUS NEIGHING** startled Earnest Pardy from his slumber.

With weary and dreary eyes, he groaned, turning over to read the bedside clock. Fumbling with his thin-framed glasses, he noted the electronic lights displaying almost two AM and muttered to himself, "Good Lord Almighty. What's gotten into those dang horses?"

Fighting back some grogginess, Earnie swung his aged legs over the bed as fast as his body would let him. Once he planted his aching feet on the wood floor, he reached for a hunting rifle leaning against the bedside table's far side. "Better not be those blasted coyotes again. I'll show 'em."

Shuffling his way through his quaint country home of over fifty years, he made it through the kitchen to the back door.

6

"Where they at?" He gazed out the windows in the door. "I'll pump every last one of 'em full of lead."

Unafraid, he exited the safety of his home.

He kept the rifle up, marching over to the rustic barn on his property.

Even though he investigated all around from his position, nothing seemed to show signs or sounds of coyotes.

*Zzzzt.*

A hole in the barn's wooden siding granted him a glimpse of a flickering flash from within.

Again, alarmed horses bellowed from their stables.

"What on *earth?*" Earnie squinted his no longer tired eyes.

He picked up the pace as he approached one of the barn's man-doors and disturbed one of the cats as he barged in. "You Simmons boys trying to pull another bug zapper prank or what?"

A disgruntled kitty chastised its owner for being woken up with some meows.

When it finished, nothing else made a sound.

"I'm not afraid to use my rifle!" Earnie readied the weapon to fire. "And if you crap yer pants, I could use the manure."

Silence filled the barn.

Over the many years, he'd honed his brave no-nonsense abilities.

Yet, in this moment, the hairs on his arms stood on end.

"No dang coyotes and no kids." He gave the barely moonlit barn interior one last lookover, shook his head, then turned back toward the door. "Checkin' the stables, then I'm gettin' my behind back in bed."

*Snap-crack-ack-ack!*

"I heard that!" Earnie swung right around with his rifle more ready than before. "Show your scrawny faces! Come on out where I can see—"

*CRRRRACK-ACK-ACK! ZAP! CRACKLE! SNAP!*

Earnie dropped the weapon.

Vibrant swirling of electrical-like energy exploded outward into existence. The chaotic sparks and crackles took circular form, whipping up dust and bits of loose hay into the air.

Stunned into standing still, Earnie said a silent prayer to himself.

The ominous window-like entity had opened to a different world.

An imposing, intimidating creature stared at him.

*"Jesus.…"* Taking one step back, Earnie forced his throat to swallow.

Curious, the prehistoric animal poked its head through the anomaly.

All Earnie could focus on—the teeth.

"You… You…s-s-stay right where you're at."

A low, rumbling growl came from the creature's chest, vibrating every board and beam throughout the barn.

"Don't you.…" Earnie had backed up into the wall beside the door he'd entered through. "Keep yourself on *that side* now. I won't bother—"

*RAOWR! R-R-RAOWR!*

A pair of small heads peered over the bottom of the electrical ring of mysterious energy. The same species as the bigger one, they vocalized to each other.

"Oh, my my." Placing a hand on his chest, Earnie gasped at the not-so-scary younglings. He'd started to grab onto the door's handle, but the current sight made him let go.

One of the baby reptilian beings hopped over the bottom of the sizzling ring.

The second one followed.

As their curiosity increased, the scaley creatures advanced even closer to the elderly human.

"No no, you shouldn't be getting closer." Earnie placed his hand back on the doorknob. "Yer momma might get—"

*ZZEEUU-POP!*

All substance of the time rift zapped into nothingness.

"Oh… Oh no," Earnie brought a trepidatious hand to his mouth. "Oh Lordy. Oh Jesus…. What am I—"

*RAAUUUU!*

One of the infant dinosaurs called out for its mother.

*RAAUUUU-RAAUUUU!*

The second one began doing the same, fearful of being separated from its family.

Overwhelmed by the crazy happenstance, Earnie did the only thing he could think of to try and calm the stranded babies.

Wincing, he got down on both knees and stretched out his shaky arms. "Come on, qui-quiet now, or you'll wake the whole barnyard. Come on now."

Focusing on his gentle coaxing, the pair of little dinosaurs took inquisitive yet cautious steps.

"That's it, lil' fellas." He smiled as he spoke. "Come see ol' Earnest."

The braver one of the infants stepped right up to him and cocked its head to study him with both eyes on the sides of its head.

Slowly, Earnie rested his quivering hand on the crown of its smooth head. "Aw, there we go. Aren't you a couple of sweeties?"

Behind the braver dinosaur, the other stayed back a few feet. It observed the non-hostile interaction between the strange human and its brethren.

Earnie brought his hand under the closer theropod's chin and proceeded to rub and scratch it. "My my my." He took a moment to look around at where the inexplicable rift once stood. He'd never been interested in science fiction books, movies, or shows. To have something like this occur right in his backyard, he shook his head trying to come to terms with it.

The second dinosaur came in a little closer.

Earnie's grin switched to uneasiness. He'd spent years caring for the usual farm animals, providing them with a proper environment and food.

As he looked at the unusual newcomers, he sighed. "Now, what in heaven's blazes am I gonna do with you two, huh?"

"Hello? Anyone home?"

A young voice pulled Earnie's attention away from the dinosaurs. "Who could that be this time of night?"

Making sure the barn door had closed behind him to

keep the creatures secure, he then hobbled over to a gate at the side of his house. "Who's there?"

Luz stepped along the wraparound porch and stopped when she came to the corner. "Oh, hello s-sir, I'm so sorry to bother you, but um—"

"Don't look familiar. Are ya lost?" Earnie had never been used to late-night visitors, and she'd become the third.

"First, this may sound crazy, but is this the year twenty-twenty-one?" Luz cringed, hoping to not seem weird.

Taking in her question and adding it to the two prehistoric creatures currently in his barn, Earnie opened his mouth, then huffed out a windy chuckle. "Lil' missy, yer time is right, but ya still seem outta place."

Wondering how far home really was, she gazed down the road. "What's the nearest town?"

"Stateside, Alpine would be the closest." He nodded to her two-wheeled form of transportation. "It's a long ways to bike out here from town."

Luz laughed to herself. "Yeah, I uh, took a little detour." She turned and pointed to her bike. "The chain on my bike is busted, and I know my parents will end me if I don't get home soo—"

*HAAAAWOOOOOOOOOOONK!*

Earnie and Luz both flinched at the sudden noise.

Across the road from them, a peculiar animal climbed out from the ditch. Its large three-toed feet crunched onto the gravel road. It swung its head both ways, checking out its surroundings.

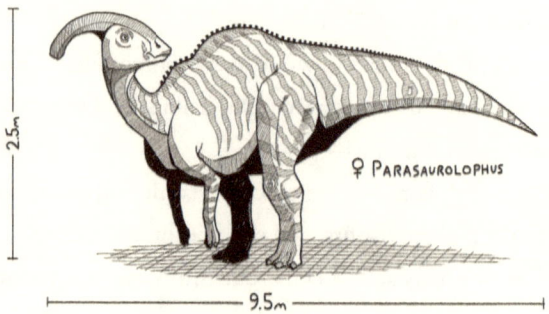

♀ PARASAUROLOPHUS

2.5m

9.5m

"Goodness. Another one?" Earnie took slow steps until he made it off the porch.

Luz noticed the crested horn coming off the back of the dinosaur's head before giving the man an odd stare. "What do you mean *'another one'?*"

Whistling with his pinkies in the crooks of his mouth, Earnie waved the creature on. "Let's get goin' now, bucko. Get off the road before you…or someone else gets hurt."

The crested dinosaur honked, making its way closer to the humans.

Luz backed up into the farmhouse's clad siding. "Whoa, are you out of your mind? You really want it around?"

Chuckling, Earnie stepped even closer as it lowered its head. "This thing just made a frightenin' trip to somewhere unfamiliar. Anyone and *anything* should feel welcome anywhere…" He patted the dinosaur on its scaley head. "…*anytime.*"

Luz lessened her squinting and embraced a small grin. Seeing an old man show so much compassion for a displaced animal struck a warm chord within her. "How about when you finish up with…this thing, could you please give me a lift home?"

Unlatching a larger gate along the wooden fence, Earnie gazed back at the girl with a nod. "I'd be happier than a duck in rain, lil' missy."

# THREE

## PRESENT DAY

**"THOUGHT I** told you not to call me on this line."

Sitting at a bar, a woman took a sip from her glass. "Just wanted you to know I'm on the inside now."

"Inside?" The man on the other end of the phone call hesitated. "Inside of what?"

"By the way, have you ever tried *biska?*" She savored the flavors once more. "It's a mistletoe-flavored brandy, I'm going to have to bring some home with—"

"Zoey, *inside of what?*"

With hints of biska on her tongue, she took a deep inhale through her nose. "Dusco Vidović. I had to speed up the lovey-dovey stuff, but he's taking me back to his place tonight."

Another pause preceded a reply. "Are you telling me you're in *Croatia* right now?"

"Relax, Sebastian, I've totally got this."

Sebastian Sharpe audibly sighed through the phone. "Listen to me, you need to get back here right—"

"He's back. Gotta run, *byeeee!*"

Picking up her glass of Croatia's finest, Zoey swiped her cellphone's camera on and pouted her lips.

Having returned from the bathroom, Dusco Vidović— her mark—leaned in, met her turquoise eyes, and kissed her.

"Baby, you ruined my picture!" Zoey giggled and kissed him back.

Dusco grabbed his jacket as he glanced around the dim-lit bar area. "But you make me so crazy about you, Zo."

About to take another sip, she frowned. "Are we leaving? Already?"

He pulled out his phone to check an incoming message, then slid it back into his pant pocket. "I have to meet a buyer."

"But I've barely started drinking my—"

"Bartender, a bottle for my girl, please." Dusco pulled out a wad of money from his inner jacket pocket. He flipped through the currency, removed some from the clip, and slid it toward the man on the other side of the bar top.

Used to doing business with Dusco, the bartender smirked and placed a biska bottle beside the cash.

Zoey grinned. "I should get you to buy me drinks more often."

Dusco grabbed the alcohol. "After I meet with this contact tonight, I'll buy you all the drinks you want."

Minutes later, Dusco pulled up in front of a run-down warehouse on the outskirts of Trieste.

Zoey glanced around at the environment. "Really digging the sketchy vibe here."

"And I need you to stay out here while I go inside."

Hand on his wrist, she stopped him from leaving the Porsche. "Nu-uh, you're not leaving me out here by myself."

"I can't take you in—"

"Fine." She ripped her hand away and tucked her arms across her chest. "Leave me here for some serial killer to grab."

Standing in the crook of the car door and the main vehicle, Dusco rolled his eyes and huffed. "Okay, okay, you can come in."

"Yaaaaaay!" Zoey hopped out and closed her passenger door. "I won't end up on a forensics TV show!" She rushed and kissed him on the cheek. "I swear, I won't get in the way."

Dusco put his hands up in a warning manner. "Just…be cool, all right?"

She stayed behind him as he marched up to a metal door.

Beside it, a garage-style door had been modified to be larger than usual. One of the outside lights attached to the corners flickered.

After straightening his jacket, Dusco banged on the door with the small end of his fist.

A few uneventful seconds passed by.

Zoey squinted at the entrance. "Isn't this where we get attacked by a *Stranger Things* monster?"

Dusco turned to give her a slightly annoyed glare. "Stranger Things?"

"Seriously? You haven't seen—"

A small speaker beside the door crackled to life with a robotic voice. *"Identification."*

With his finger on a button, Dusco responded, "Vidović, Dusco."

The speaker replayed his voice and name, then added, *"Verified. Enter."*

A mechanism within the door unlocked.

Dusco held the door open for his tag-along.

"Ooooooh, it's like you and I are *Totally Spies* right now." Zoey stepped inside onto a concrete floor. "Only I'd look better in the jumpsuit."

"Quiet, Zo."

The door closed behind them.

Zoey continued taking careful steps inside until she came to a reflective wall. Placing a hand on the cool surface, she noted the murky hue. "Dusco, what is—"

A hefty aquatic figure swam past, barely visible.

*"Do not touch!"* Another Croatian man hollered as he entered the large room. "Unless you have outbid me. Dusco, should she be here with—"

"Don't mind her," Dusco responded without worry. "She's just…had a bit to drink."

"This…" Zoey backed up a bit. "…is a fish tank?"

Dusco chuckled. *"Fish."*

Once more, the creature within the aquarium approached the glass closest to the humans. Slowing down, it gave everyone a better look at its mouth lined with seven-inch-long teeth.

Its dark eyes pierced Zoey to her core.

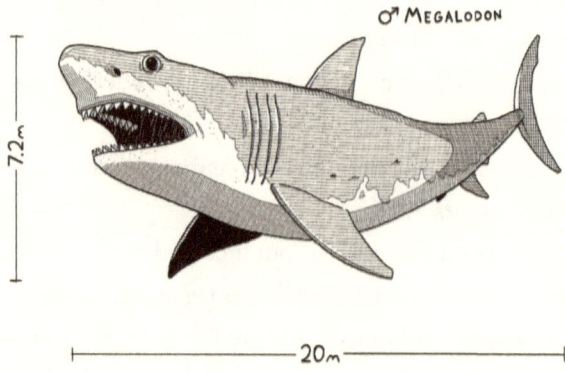

♂ Megalodon

7.2ₘ

20ₘ

The other guy pulled out his phone, considered Zoey being American, and spoke in Croatian. "Transfer for the megalodon is ready, Dusco."

"*Hvala vam,* Tomislav." He placed his cellphone closer to the buyer's, and grinned when the acceptance notification came in. "Good business."

Tomislav laughed. "This young megalodon is a business in itself. The teeth…" he slipped his phone back into his pocket as he approached his acquisition. "…they will produce a small fortune. Keep pulling them out, and they will regrow until it dies."

Zoey finally pulled her gaze away from the prehistoric creature. "That's so inhumane."

Dusco didn't look up from his phone, already dividing his money into separate accounts. "Is not your problem, Zo."

"Actually, it is."

"Dusco." Tomislav snorted. "Who the heck *is* this *girl?*"

Zoey swiped Sebastian's contact left on her phone to text

him:

**My position. Megalodon juvie. 2 minutes.**

She slipped the phone back into her pant pocket, then cocked her head to the side as she approached the buyer. "Sorry, Tomislav, my animal activist senses were tingling."

"These creatures don't even belong here." He shrugged as he spoke. "Which means, what happens to them is no matter."

She stood a couple of feet away from him and stared.

Her glare made Tomislav uncomfortable. "What are you doing? Stop it."

Zoey raised her voice. "You're wearing *a wire,* aren't you?"

Dusco looked up from his cellphone. "A wire?" He stomped over, slipping his gun out from under his jacket. "Tomislav, who do you work—"

*Slap! Click-Click!*

In a swift movement, Zoey handcuffed the two men together and wrenched the gun from Dusco's hand. Backing up, she kept the gun on them. "One step or move and I'll shoot."

They raised their hands, including the cuffed ones.

Zoey kept her voice firm. "Toss your phones over."

The Croatians glanced at each other.

*BLAM!*

She shot at the ceiling. *"Now!"*

Cowering, they awkwardly lowered their phones and kicked them over.

Collecting them, Zoey backed up to a ladder attached to

the side of the tank. After climbing to the top, she gazed into the megalodon's containment tank. "And I forgot to bring a swimsuit."

Tomislav let out baffled laugh. "What is she doing?"

"She's crazy." Dusco couldn't take his eyes off her.

Once she'd taken a breath to calm her nerves, Zoey dove right in. Opening her eyes underwater, the megalodon's head passed right by her. After taking a moment to fully comprehend what she had to do, she swam toward the prehistoric shark.

The megalodon swam to the furthest end from her, then turned and picked up speed.

Zoey popped her head above the water, sucking in a deep breath.

Its dorsal fin broke through the surface.

She treaded, bracing for impact.

As its head came within a couple feet of her, she brought an arm above water.

*Thwack!*

Punching it in the gills, Zoey snagged the top fin with both hands as the megalodon flinched. She held on, clenching the fin as the creature thrashed.

Dusco's jaw dropped in complete bafflement. "Is she riding—"

*ZEEUU-ZEEUU-ZEEUU-BWOOOOOOOOM!*

# FOUR

**"SERIOUSLY, I** don't even know what to say to you right now." Sebastian Sharpe sat at his desk across from a damp Zoey.

"'Great job saving the megalodon, Zoey'?" She wiped some water from behind her left ear. "'Thanks for stopping another dino deal, Zoey.' Or how about, 'Because of your help, we now have access to more files and contacts in the prehistoric black market.'?"

About to counter concerning his worries, he cocked an eyebrow. "*More* files and contacts?"

Zoey revealed the two phones belonging to the Croatian men, setting them on her side of the desk. "At least those two schmoes were smart enough to get water-proof smartphones."

Sebastian tapped on the screen of one of them, lighting it up. Another piece of the intel puzzle had landed in his lap. "This...."

She wore a proud grin. "Sound it out with me now. Thhhh-aaaa-nnnn-kkkk—"

"You could've been killed. These people...they don't play nice." He crossed his arms, observing overgrown jungle through his office window. His base of operations existed on a time-displaced prehistoric island in the Bermuda Triangle. "And that would've left the blood of *two Beaumonts* on my hands."

All cocky rebuttals Zoey had lined up disappeared with the mention of her mother.

Sebastian rubbed his face before breaking the somber silence. "Listen, I'm sorry, Zo. That came out—"

"My mom *chose* to work with you, and that led to her death. I get it." She stared at the desk, losing herself in the darkness of its wood grain. "Which is why I *need* to be doing this."

With a warmer tone, he tried to meet her gaze, "By putting yourself in the same kind of danger?"

A tiny self-assured laugh escaped her nose. "If it means taking down the kind of people that killed her, then *yes.*"

Needing to release anxious energy in his legs, Sebastian stood up and walked right up to the window. He slid one of the panes open, which disturbed a pair of oversized dragonflies on the building's exterior. "I know we've talked about her before, but Dawn really was one of the best."

Zoey picked up on the guilt in his voice. "Arrowsmith killed her. Not you."

A long exhale exited his lungs. "Seems like everyone I get involved with becomes endangered in some way or another.

Kam and Viv, your mom, Feli...." Saying Felicia's name caught his throat and summoned tears to his eyes. "She... She barely survived. I was so close to losing—"

"*Seb.*" Zoey immediately got up and came to his side. "The only ones that knew of that car bomb were the horrible people that put it there."

"And what if something horrible happens to *you?*"

Placing a hand on his shoulder, she joined him in gazing out the window as tears trickled down her cheeks. "If my mom was one of the best, then that best is in my DNA, too."

Sebastian managed a small chuckle. "Which means?"

"Meaning...." She gave his shoulder a squeeze while forcing a deep breath into her lungs. "I'm your new *MVDSP.*"

Throwing his head back into a snort-laugh, he shook his head as he looked at her. "What the heck does that even mean?"

She infused more confidence into her voice. "Most valuable dinosaur saving personnel."

"You're a wildcard," he countered, giving her shoulder a light punch. "And I still can't believe you dove into a tank with a megalodon."

Zoey laughed, going over the recent solo mission in her head. "I can't believe I actually punched it, or else—"

A buzzing came from the desk.

Sebastian left the window to pick up his cellphone. Text messages had come through, notifying him of some of his operations in progress. Looking up from the phone, he noticed Zoey soaking up the gorgeous view from his office. Since the day he told her of Dawn's demise, it had become clear to him that passion and determination were Beaumont traits.

Traits that he fully respected and admired.

Back to reading the messages, he raised his voice. "Ever been to Texas?"

Zoey pulled her attention away from the vibrant greens and ancient vegetation. "It's been a while, got some distant family there. Why do you ask?"

Sebastian finished typing a reply and sent it. "My sources are closing in on someone who's been smuggling creatures into Mexico, but it's been a little tricky for them."

She gave him an expectant stare. "What are you saying, Seb?"

He grinned. "I'm saying…they may need a *wildcard*."

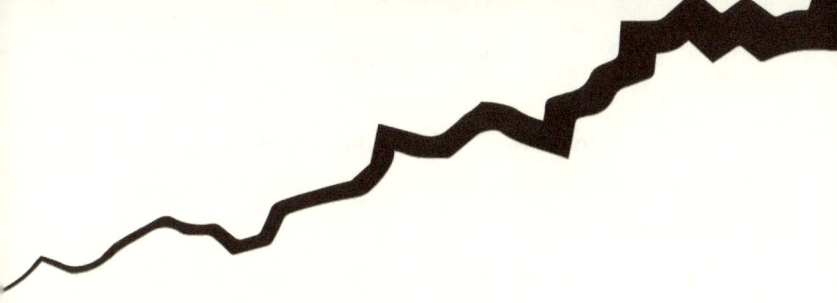

# FIVE

**"AND IF** you're new here, hi my name is Ally and my partner Matt is off-screen, we are *The Mysterious Bookcase!* We're a U.K.-based business where you can order pre-loved and newer books in the style of 'blind date with a book'. We also have a supervisor, Harry, our kitty-floof, who is goofing around here somewhere...."

Sketching away at her desk, Lucero Sanchez kept a Live video running on her tablet.

*Buzzzz. Buzzzz.*

She glanced at her cellphone, looked at who had messaged her, then returned to adding detail around the creature's eyes.

On the Live video, the owner Ally responded to viewers. "Yes, Shannen and Lainey, we have read the new book Saura-Portal by Kamren Eckhardt, isn't it amazing?"

In the background, Matt piped up. "And we currently have copies available in our online indie bookshop."

Ally continued with, "We love this new take on dinosaurs and time travel. I'm a big kid at heart, and I absolutely loved it!"

Zavier, Luz's older brother, popped his head through her doorway and attempted a raspy English accent. "As the wild Lucero sits in her natural habitat, her favorite pastime is combining her name alongside the boy she's in love wi—"

*Plunk!*

A pen struck him in the side of the head.

"Do you *mind,* Zav?" Luz fired a glare at him before returning to her picture.

"Hey, that better not leave a mark." He rubbed his right cheekbone. "I've got a date with Yesenia tomorrow."

"At least *one of us* will have a date then."

Zav narrowed his gaze at her. "What does that mea…. Wait, did Ollie break up with you?"

*Buzzzz. Buzzzz.*

Luz didn't look up from her sketchbook. A single tear dropped onto the paper, blotting some of her pencilwork.

"Is that Ollie right now?" Zav finally stepped into the room, pulling out his own phone, ready to defend her honor. "I'll tell him to go straight to—"

"It isn't him," she whimpered.

"*Qué?*"

"It *isn't him,* Zavier…."

Hearing the break in her voice, Zav came closer to her side. "Why aren't you answering?"

"Because…." Gripping her pencil tighter, she shuddered while sucking in a breath. "He…*left me*…for *Daira.*"

His eyes opened wide. Opening his mouth, he took a moment to string the right words together. He had to take into consideration that Luz and Daira had been best friends for the better part of a decade. "She's the one messaging you?"

"And I'm not answering."

Knowing the two girls loved each other like sisters, he placed a hand on Luz's shoulder. "Maybe she wants to—"

"*I am not answering her.*"

Nodding while giving her shoulder a squeeze, Zav pulled away. He looked down to her sketchbook and changed the subject. "Are you drawing another...something? Is that even a dinosaur? A mega...ther-what?"

♀ MEGATHERIUM

Luz took a moment to wipe her cheeks. "It's a prehistoric mammal called a megatherium. Basically, the largest sloth to ever—"

"*Okay,* I get it, you're still a nerd," he responded with a chuckle. Heading back to the doorway, he stopped and spun back around. "Am I still taking you to Earnie's tomorrow morning for your horse-riding lessons?"

The mention of heading to Earnie's brought a smile to her

face. "Just in case, I'll call and see if this weekend still works."

Once her brother left and she heard his footsteps take him to the kitchen, she picked up her cellphone. The screen lit up. Daira's texts took her entire focus. About to tap on them, Luz entered her passcode and ignored the messages.

She opened her call history, tapped on Earnie's contact, and tucked the phone between her ear and shoulder.

A couple of rings later, the elderly man answered, "Ol' Earnie here in your ear."

Luz chuckled at his intro. "Hey, Earnie. How's my favorite oldie-but-goodie doing today?"

"Any better and I couldn't stand it," he answered with an audible smile.

She half-rolled her eyes at his usual-yet-charming response. "Does this weekend still work for some…'*horse riding lessons*'?"

Earnie picked up on their code word and snickered. "Sure it does, lil' missy!" He cleared his throat and lowered his voice. "Also, the sauropelta, uh…. Am I saying that right?"

"Feels like I'm teaching everyone phonics today. Sore-oh-pel-tah," Luz sounded out. "You were so close."

"Right, the spikey one," he laughed back. "Some of her clutch started hatching today. Gon' need some help naming the little ones."

Luz sucked in an excited breath and flexed her fingers. "I'll start writing some down right now! Ahhhh, that's so exciting, I can't wait!"

"Listen, Alvaro, I'm good for any shipments you need for next week, but this weekend is for me and my kids." Humberto Sanchez spoke through the Bluetooth setup in his pickup truck.

"Thought you said you *needed the money*," Alvaro, his work associate, countered.

"*Sí,* but I'm already behind on this one," Humberto responded with exasperation. "And as long as I can keep this one asleep with the temperature regulators, I desperately need some sleep so I—"

"The only day the recipients have available for the cargo is Sunday."

Humberto shook his head, as it had already turned into Friday night. "You don't understand, that's *the day* that—"

"From what I *understand,* you don't want to *provide* for your family," Alvaro shot back, lacking all sympathy.

An audible sigh slipped through Humberto's nose.

Alvaro took the silence as a hesitant agreement. "I'll put you down for Sunday, then."

*Click.*

Once the phone call ended, Humberto squeezed the steering wheel tighter. Caring for Zavier and Lucero as a single father since Hana had died close to a year ago came with its challenges. With her loss, the rest of the family had lost its glue, rock, and heart. Lately, Humberto feared he'd been losing his grip on his kids. Unfortunately, anyone who turned down a cartel job would be considered as unreliable. *Of all the days, it* had *to be on a Sunday.*

About to turn onto the street to take him home, he did

his best to come up with an excuse to tell them. Something to keep them in the dark, and not allude to the fact he'd been working for a particular cartel for the past six months.

After pulling into the driveway, he immediately exited the truck and ran into the garage for a heavy-duty extension cord. He connected up to the containment trailer, in case a backup source of power would be needed. In a crouched position to plug the cord in, he gave the side of the trailer a pat before standing back up.

"Usually you call when—"

"*Gaaaah!*" Humberto spun on his heels, stepped on the cord—pulling it out of the socket just enough—while throwing his hands up before realizing his daughter had come outside to see him. "Luz—*Dios mío*—don't sneak up on me like that."

Giggling, Luz lifted her arms and wrapped herself around him. "I missed you, *Papi.*"

"Same, *mija.*" He gave her a tight squeeze back and kissed the top of her head. "How was your day today? Is Zav inside?"

She leaned into him as they walked up to the side door. "School was your typical 'will I actually use this information in life?', Ollie dumped me, and I think Zav is inside playing video—"

"Did you just say Ollie broke up with you?" Humberto turned and placed his hands on her shoulders. "Want me to put the fear of God into him?"

Luz snorted. "I see where Zav gets his protectiveness from." She gazed down at the stone path leading up to the door. "And no, I'll…work through it."

Right at that moment, Humberto saw his late wife in his daughter. He placed a hand under her chin and gave her a reassuring grin. "Listen, Luz, I know mothers are usually better at helping their daughters through things like this, and I…may not know exactly what to say, but…."

They both looked down to the ground, searching the blades of grass and pebbles for the perfect words.

"I… really needed her today," Luz managed to squeak out.

Humberto touched his forehead to hers. "Same, *mija*."

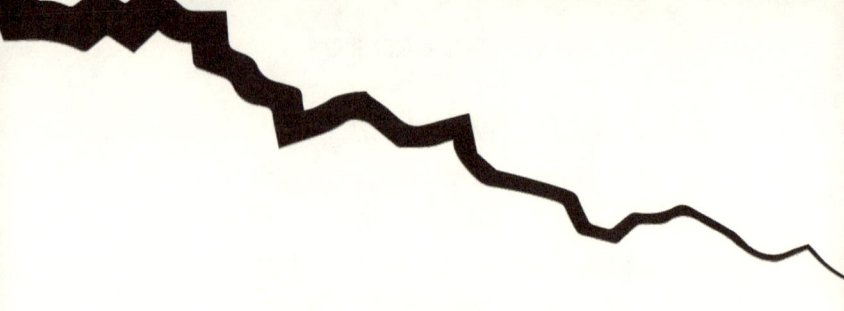

# SIX

**"BEFORE WE** show you the money, show us the dinosaurs."

In a semi-hidden area among a shipyard in the Corpus Christi port of Texas, a clandestine swap for goods had brought two groups of nefarious criminals together.

On one side, a Mexican cartel would receive prehistoric animals.

As for the American party, they expected a massive payday.

Izan, one of the cartel's lieutenants, glanced around at his crew. "They better have made the trip all in one piece, Mr. Garrett. My superior wasn't happy with the last couple of shipments."

"Don't get your Spanish panties in a bunch." Standing in front of four custom-made shipping containers, the man surnamed Garrett surveyed his covert team tending to and preparing them. "From the left, a pack of four dire wolves, one adolescent diabloceratops, a pair of nan...nanuqsauruses—who came up with these freaking names?—and the last has three kapro... Uh, kaprosu... kaprosuchuses?"

Wary, Izan squinted. "All in good condition?"

Garrett nodded. "Our best people checked on them during transport." He slipped a tablet out of a protective case, entered a passcode, then turned it toward the Mexican contact.

Four video feeds displayed the creature contents of each container.

Pacing up and down their metallic prison, the dire wolves seemed restless.

As for the crocodilian-like kaprosuchuses, they hissed as built-in sprinklers sprayed a mist, keeping them moisturized.

The diabloceratops slumbered in its chamber.

After giving them a once-over, the clean-shaven Izan lessened his skeptical stare. "Looks good to me. Ortiz, give these men their payment."

A tank of a man lifted two briefcases off the back of a suped-up pickup truck. Making his way to them, he didn't even flinch over the weight of money in his possession.

"What kind of fajitas are you feeding your men these days?" Garrett took a step back as the cases were dropped a couple feet away from him.

"Just take your money, *amigo.*"

Compliant, Garrett became more energized as he reached for the case's handles. "I'm just saying, I might need some of that *special* hot sauce myself—"

*Clink-ka-tink-clink!*

Multiple heads swiveled.

Dario gazed off to the right and pointed.

Dropping the cases, Garrett whipped an arm up to his face. "Flash grenade!"

*KA-BOOOOM!*

Ringing entered everyone's ears.

Garrett stumbled to his knees.

Cartel members struggled to arm themselves.

Multiple unidentified personnel stormed the operation with rifles ready and shouting instructions to each other.

"Everyone, *get down* on the ground!" One built man in particular marched over to the main drop point, pushed Garrett the rest of the way to the ground, and waved his gun around. "Don't even think about reaching for anything, Izan."

Mustering some strength, Garrett pushed himself up and into the operative. Launching a left punch into his opponent's abs, he swung for the head with his right.

With a quick-raised bent elbow, the man blocked the incoming fist with an annoyed grunt and immediately rammed his open palm into Garrett's throat. Sweeping out his right leg, he returned Garrett to the hard ground.

Noticing Izan turning to run, the operative recalled the mission required everyone to be alive.

*BLAM-CRACK!*

"*Gaaaauuuugh!*" Kneecapped by the bullet, Izan crumbled. "Who are... How did you know about—"

"Been tracking this deal for a while now." Keeping

everything at a no-nonsense approach, the mystery man pulled out a set of handcuffs. "Background checks are great. Should try them on your own people sometime."

Special Ops arrivals relieved all targets of their weapons.

Vertical to the ground, Garrett spat out, "Who even are you guys?"

"Evander Evers." He ended his introduction with a click of the cuffs. "SauraCorps thanks you for your compliance."

Flat on the ground, another cartel member slowly pulled a fob of sorts out of his pocket.

One of Evander's men noticed at the last second. "Hey! Toss that right—"

*Beeeep!*

Every door to each containment unit buzzed as they unlocked.

Alarmed, Evander began barking orders. "Prep with tranqs, and *watch those doors!*" He marched over to the man with the fob. "And you, Vidales, right? Hand it over before I break your—"

A wild toss sent the handheld gadget under one of the units.

Evander scowled as he cracked his neck. "Frig sakes."

*RAAAAAA-UUUUUUGH!*

Two SauraCorps operatives pressed their body weight into a pair of metal doors.

*WHA-BANG!*

Both men went flying as a pale-skinned nanuqsaurus pushed itself through, followed by the second one. Half the size of a tyrannosaurus rex, their teeth still gave them an intimidating presence.

"Take them *down, now!*" Evander finished cuffing Vidales.

A deep grumble came from the unit right behind them.

Crumpling the doors as it charged, the diabloceratops—with two long curved horns at the top of its frill—charged straight at them.

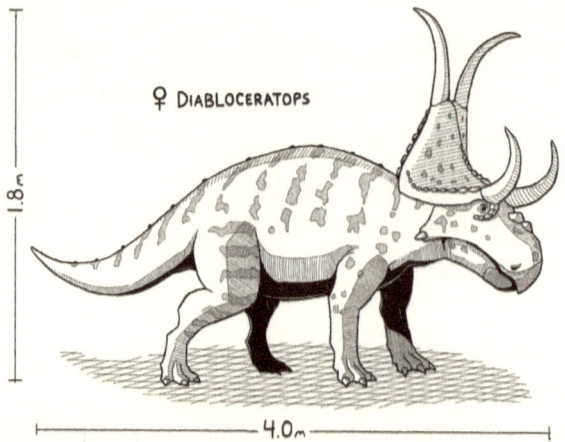

♀ DIABLOCERATOPS

1.8m

4.0m

Evander rolled off to the side, pulling Vidales with him. Springing back up, he reached into a cargo pant leg pocket.

The startled diabloceratops drove its front feet into the ground as it turned and locked onto him.

*GRRUUUUAAAAAAW!*

It bolted for him.

Starting to run in a zig-zag, Evander managed to keep it off him for a couple seconds as he loaded his gun with different ammo. Narrowly missing a strike from its head, he careened back toward it and grabbed onto the side of its frill.

His foot nearly slipped as he shoved off from its left shoulder and up higher behind its frill.

Shuddering to a halt, the diabloceratops began swaying its head back and forth, trying to shake the human off of it.

Evander hung onto one of the top horns with one arm, but a sudden jolt sent his forehead into the other.

His weapon fell.

"Bucking bronco, huh?" He clung as hard as possible with his one arm as he fumbled a hand into his inner jacket pocket. "Show me...what you got!"

Agitated, the dinosaur bucked, shook its entire body, and wobbled its head side to side.

Learning its pattern, Evander lessened his grip on the horn and swung himself around to land on its head.

A small jerk slid him down further.

He came eye to eye with the beast.

"Nighty-night!"

Evander slipped further down and slammed a syringe into its neck.

*GRUAAAAAAH! GRUU...aaaah.*

Thrown from its head, Evander tucked and rolled, and took up cover behind one of the surrounding shipping containers.

Eventually, the diabloceratops gave in to the tranquilizer and stumbled into a deep sleep.

Getting his breathing back to a proper rhythm, Evander gazed over at his crew. One of the nanuqsauruses had already been downed as the second one took a tranq dart to its abdomen and roared at the humans. He checked the third container where another two SauraCorps operatives kept the dire wolves inside. "Of course they all got the *easy* ones."

Finding his gun, he picked it up and looked to where he'd rolled with Vidales.

Gone.

He holstered the weapon with an exasperated grunt. "Dammit."

Having taken care of everyone involved in the dinosaur deal, Evander strolled up to one of the dinosaur containment units. "Cargo's all good?"

One of the vet techs had finished their check-ups. "All *animals* vitals are satisfactory, and should be ready for transport."

Evander picked up on the desired term. "Animals, cargo, same thing."

The veterinarian scoffed. "How'd your attitude win you a job with SauraCorps?"

"Attitude ain't got nothing to do with it," he retorted, pulling out his cellphone. "Getting the job done is what got me the job." Turning away, he opened up the phone to a text.

Going back to his paperwork, the scientist snorted. "*Ain't?* Thought SauraCorps dealt with *dinosaurs,* not *Neanderthals.*"

Evander spun around one second later, pushing the scientist into the large shipping container's metal wall. "Calling me *stupid,* huh, doc?"

Others from the team yelled at Evander to back down.

Shaking, the vet winced. "I-I-I'm sorry, I didn't—"

"Let's have a little experiment of our own, shall we?" Evander wore a sinister grin. "My hypothesis: if I shove this phone down your throat, you won't be able to—"

*Buzzzz. Buzzzz.*

Evander uttered a disappointed grunt. "Saved by the ringtone." Letting go of the veterinarian's bunched up shirt, he cracked his neck as he headed back toward his vehicle. "Evening, Sharpe."

On the other end, Sebastian sat up straighter even in Evander's voice presence. "Evers, I take it the sting operation went well."

"As well as could be."

"Nobody died?"

"Had to kneecap one of them 'cause he tried to run." Evers chuckled to himself. "I love it when they run."

"*Again?*" Sebastian put a hand to his mouth. "If I had a nickel for *every time* you've kneecapped someone—"

"Knees were meant for bending and bullets."

About to tell him, '*You need therapy*', Sebastian opted to move past it. "Anyway, I've got a new operation for you. And you're actually not that far."

"I'm game." Evander hopped in his SUV. "Send me the specs."

Sebastian smirked. "But first, I need you to pick someone up from the airport tomorrow morning."

# SEVEN

**HUMBERTO ALWAYS** cherished family dinner. Leaving the stress of work behind him, he savored every moment he could spend with his kids. Being with them always gave him something nothing else could: a smile on his face, and love in his heart.

Zavier became animated as he retold a story from class. "And when Mr. Kroeger's back was turned, Chuck threw his lunch bag up into the ceiling fan."

Lucero had already been belly laughing. "No, wait, why didn't you already tell me this?"

"But the *best part*...." Zav took a moment, catching his breath. "Somehow, the fan caught the zipper on the bottom..."

Humberto's shoulders bounced as he chuckled. "Oh noooo."

"...*unzipping* the storage part..."

Luz's eyes started to water. "It did not!"

"...it opened *all the way*, sending the mini pretzels flying *everywhere!*" Zav rocked in his chair, unable to contain himself.

Raising her hands into the air, Luz separated them as if posting the word in the air. "Epic."

"And no one got caught?" Humberto shook his head, laughing at the absurdity of it all. "You guys should really watch yourselves."

Zav snorted. "Kroeger simply can't handle kids. He shouldn't be teaching at all."

Humberto squinted, pausing in thought. "How do you know he isn't dealing with something behind closed doors? Maybe your class is adding to his already stressful life, he could even be depressed, and he has to face your difficult class every single day."

Both kids quieted down as they considered the possibility.

Humberto broke the silence. "We all wish people would take it easy on us when we're having hard days." He lowered his gaze to the last of his shrimp taco with mango salsa on his plate. "But life is messy, and easy is in short supply these days."

"It was just a silly prank." Zav took a sip of his orange pop.

Reaching over, Humberto covered his son's hand with his own. "I know, *mijo.* Just remember how you had hard days when your mother passed."

Luz finally piped back up. "I wasn't myself at all."

"Exactly." Taking a look at his kids, Humberto decided to stop bringing things down. "But tomorrow, we're going to have *fun!* We can watch *Robin Hood: Men in Tights*, I'll make our spicy popcorn and snacks, and—"

"Zav's taking me to 'grandpa' Earnie's tomorrow morning," Luz brought up with regret in her eyes.

Taken out of his excitement, Humberto sat back in his chair. "Oh...for your horse riding lessons, right?"

"And he just got a brand-new saddle for me to try out," she added, hoping her father would let her still go. "He said I could stay until Sunday, too."

The mention of that particular day made Humberto nod. "I, uh... have another dispatch job on Sunday, anyway."

Luz and Zav looked to each other, giving the same look of '*Another job?*'

All three of them glanced around, unsure of what to say to make things less disheartening.

*Buzzzz. Buzzzz.*

Humberto exhaled as he left the table and picked up his cellphone. Accepting the call, he opened with, "*Sí?*"

"Emergency meeting, now."

"What? *Por qué?*"

"The deal at Corpus Christi got busted," the other person answered. "Someone's onto us, and we need to discuss new options."

Rubbing his forehead, Humberto looked back to his kids. They needed him to be there, but they also needed provisions to live a comfortable life.

Imagining Hana sitting at the table, he recalled some of her words before she passed away: *I have faith that when I'm gone, as long as Zav and Luz have you in their lives, our family will survive.*

One word stuck out to him.

*Survive.*

Closing his eyes, he clenched his teeth together. "Where are we meeting?"

Leaning against the front doorway, Luz watched as her dad drove off with one of his coworkers. After getting the phone call, his demeanor had changed completely. She'd seen him mask his feelings before, but this time, he'd been beyond unsettled.

Holding her phone in one hand, she mulled over reading her best friend Daira's messages.

Her father's words at dinner rolled through her brain like waves lapping onto a beach.

*…Life is messy, and easy is in short supply…*

Squeezing her eyes shut, she sat down on the front porch.

Forcing herself to open her phone, she discovered four texts from Daira waiting for her.

Her thumb hovered over the conversation block.

*WHA-BANG!*

Startled and glancing around, she tried to find the source.

None of the neighbors had anything going on.

*HI-I-I-I-I-I-I-I-I-ISSSS!*

She immediately locked onto her dad's heavy-duty trailer that he'd unhitched earlier when he arrived. "What the heck?"

Its wheels shifted in the gravel.

The trailer swayed side to side.

Slipping her phone into a pant pocket, she took hesitant steps toward the ominous containment trailer. *What in the world is in there?*

A low, guttural growl reverberated through the trailer's walls.

As the strange being continued making noise, Luz brought herself to the main access door on the end.

*CLANG!*

*HI-I-I-I-I-I-I-I-I-ISSSS!*

Gazing up at a small panel with buttons, she pondered one last question as she reached out. *What is my dad actually up to?*

Her thumb connected with a green button.

Reinforced clamps clicked open around the door's edge.

It hissed open, joining in the creature's cries.

"Luz! What are you doing?" Zav pushed her out of the way, getting better access to the panel. "You can't just—"

*HI-I-I-I-I-I-I-I-I-ISSSS!*

A muzzled reptilian snout forced its way through the gap in the door.

"Oh my *Gooood!*" Zav began screaming at what she'd just unleashed. "What is *thaaaat?*"

As her brother lost his mind, Luz ended up grinning as her eyes sparked with excitement.

Zav tried to hit the red button to make the door close up again. "Luz, come on, help me close—"

*CRUNCH-SMAAAASH!*

The creature's weight drove the door to the ground,

forming a ramp. About to take a step, it jerked back. Restraints attached to the inside of the trailer kept it confined. It stumbled side to side, trying to regain balance.

"*Whooooa.*" Luz backed up, giving the freed animal some space. "Zav, get back here and shut up, you'll wake the neighbors!"

"Why are you so freaking *calm?*" he screamed back at her. "It's a-a-a—"

"Dinosaur," she announced, in absolute awe. "Spinosaurus."

♀ SPINOSAURUS

4.3ᴍ

12.2ᴍ

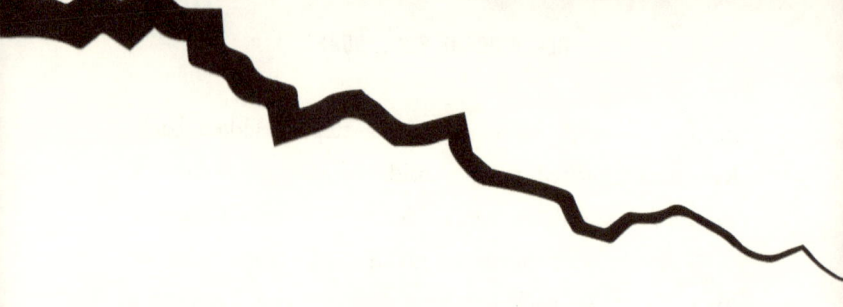

# EIGHT

**"WHY IS** there a *spinosaurus* in *Dad's trailer?*" Zavier couldn't stop staring at the intimidating creature. "I…can't believe that sentence just left my mouth."

"Didn't you know? Dad's working for *Jurassic Park… World…*whatever they're calling it now." Lucero stood at the end of the door-ramp, taking in the dinosaur's details. "You're so beautiful, or…handsome?"

Its silvery hide glistened thanks to the trailer's interior lighting. Mixes of yellows and oranges marked around its eyes, and accented the edge of the sail on its back.

Zav gave his sister a perplexed stare. "Luz."

She made her way up the ramp.

"Luz, what the heck?"

Oblivious to his concerns, she made it up to the opening. "You must be hungry, huh?"

"*Luz!*"

She spun around. "What's your problem?"

"My problem, is that you clearly *don't* have a problem with all this," he shot back. The size of the dinosaur plus the teeth lining its long, muzzled snout, had been more than enough for him to keep his distance. "Why are you acting all fine?"

Giving the spinosaurus a closer look, she noted a few black scorch marks on its left side. As if someone had prodded and forced it into the chamber. *Burns.* She met eyes with it. "It's afraid."

"Afraid?" Zav used a mocking tone. "Is it about to crap its pants? Because I am."

Luz reached up to the side of the protective muzzle. "What did they do to you, huh?" Getting her fingers on one of the clips, she let the strap fall before getting a better grip to remove it. "Let's get this thing off."

As soon as the muzzle slipped off, the spinosaurus opened its mouth wide.

*HI-I-I-I-I-I-I-I-I-ISSSS!*

Zav fell backward, even though he'd stayed out of its reach. "Dammit, Luz!"

"It's okay, it's okay!" Luz pushed past a moment of fear, rushed to the animal's neck, and placed her palms on its smooth scales. "Calm. Calm now, come on."

At this point, Zav realized he hadn't been getting through to his sister. "Luz, how are you acting so normal about this?"

Accepting the interaction from the friendly human girl, the spinosaurus closed its eyes as it released a low grumble.

Luz looked back at her brother, but didn't say a word.

Zav scrunched his eyebrows together. "I asked you a

question."

She turned her attention back to the dinosaur. Her answer would only produce more questions. "I promised... I can't tell anyone about it, not even *you*."

Back on his feet, Zav pointed to the prehistoric creature. "Clearly Dad's been keeping a secret from us. Are you keeping it, too? Have you known about this *the whole time* and—"

"Okay, whoa, wait a sec," she countered, taking a hand off the spinosaurus to hold it up in defense. "First off, I had no idea Dad was...transporting dinosaurs, or whatever this is linked to. Secondly...."

Zav waited for five seconds before hassling her again. "I'm waiting."

*HI-I-I-I-I-I-I-I-I-ISSSS!*

The spinosaurus lowered its head, tired of fighting against its restraints.

Luz noted the pain and fatigue in its eyes. She brought her cheek up to the dinosaur's, and ran her hand down the top of its snout. "It's afraid, it needs help, and a place where it can roam free."

Zav blinked rapidly at her. "And where do you suggest we take it?"

She took a deep breath, then finally stepped away from the spinosaurus. "How fast can you hook this trailer up to your truck?"

"What—are you—it's—you can't...." Unable to form a cohesive sentence, he finally came out with, "Are you *completely* out of your freaking mind?"

She marched down the ramp straight to her brother and put her hands on his shoulders. "Forget tomorrow morning. We need to get this to Earnie's right now."

As she walked away from him, Zav thought his head would explode from all the new questions now forming in his brain. "Earnie's? What's he gonna do with a dinosaur?"

Luz stopped as she opened the front door to their house. "Just you wait and see."

# NINE

**ALREADY ON** their way to Earnie's, Zavier drove his black pickup truck while Lucero opted to stay in the trailer with the spinosaurus. They decided to keep their phones on a continuous call.

Still in awe of the ancient beast, Luz enjoyed keeping it company. "Hey, Zav, did you know spinosaurus fossils have been found in Egypt and the U.K.?"

Zav wiped some sweat from his brow. "Did you know dinosaur facts do nothing to calm my nerves?"

Smirking at his quip, she hoped to at least fill some dead air between them. "Listen, I know towing a dinosaur to Earnie's isn't what you expected to be doing at nine-thirty at night. But like I said, it'll make more sense when we get there."

"Just a regular Friday for you, huh?"

"Something like tha—*ugh*." She stabilized herself after they hit a slight dip in the road. "Do you…remember that day when Earnie brought me home because I got '*lost*'?"

He squinted in response. "You haven't really talked about that day much."

Checking on a thawing fish from their house freezer, Luz figured it would be good enough to offer to the spinosaurus. "I never told you guys that…I actually rode my bike through a time rift."

It took him a moment to process her sentence. "Like, on *purpose?*"

"Yes, I saw a big scary electrical circle in the road and thought, you know what would be so much fun?" She stood up, found her road-legs, and shimmied up to the spinosaurus' head. "There was some crazy stuff going on, though. A triceratops—or it could've been a styracosaurus—anyway, it chased me. But I also saw a bunch of people back then, couldn't make out who any of them were, though."

"What? You mean *cavemen?*" Zav put his signal on to turn. "Turning left, brace yourself."

"No, modern people, they had cars, guns, and—" Luz dropped the slimy fish and ducked as the change in direction made the bulky dinosaur sway to the side. Nearly getting pinned against the trailer wall, she took an extra moment on the floor to compose herself. "*Jeez.* Solita almost crushed me."

"Who's Soli…." Zav sighed. "You named it."

"Maybe."

He chuckled. "You're weird."

"Says the guy who freaks out over a dinosaur."

"And you're still weird for being so chill about it."

Luz brought the fish up to Solita's nose, letting it identify the food first. "Does that smell good?" When Solita the spinosaurus opened its mouth, Luz tossed the fish in. "Hope this will hold you over for a bit."

*HI-I-I-I-I-I-I-I-I-ISSSS!*

Patting her on the neck, Luz grinned. "You're welcome, Solita."

Zav picked up on the eating noises. "Uh, Luz, what's she crunching on?"

She laughed before answering. "Didn't really need this foot, anyway."

"*¡Ay, Chihuahua!* Don't do that to me."

Another hour passed, with less conversation as they went along, and they finally reached Earnie's ranch. Zavier backed up to a large fence gate, then parked and headed around to open the trailer door.

As the ramp finished forming, Lucero hopped out and hurried over to Earnie's front door. She smirked at the jazzy *Let the Good Times Roll* by Ray Charles playing from the record player, rang the doorbell, and rushed back over to the restrained dinosaur. "He should be out any minute, might be dancing on his way over."

Zav leaned against the wooden fence, glancing around before glueing his gaze to the spinosaurus. "Are you still one-hundred-percent sure you want to unleash this thing?"

"She didn't attack me all the way here." Already unhooking some of the heavy-duty straps, she made her way to one of the back legs. "Solita will feel more at home once she's past that gate, you'll see."

"Especially when she attacks Earnie's horses," he countered, foreseeing nothing but a slaughter-filled ranch.

Unclipping another fetter, she glanced back and grinned. "You mean *that* horse?"

Zav turned his head, finding a large dinosaur opening its duck-billed mouth.

*HAAAAWOOOOOOOOOOONK!*

A high-pitched scream came out of Zav as he sprang forward and stumbled to the grass. "What in the *mother-loving…* What is—great, now I've literally peed myself!"

Luz laughed as the parasaurolophus honked its greeting. "Evening, Peggy. Good job on scaring him, considering you're an herbivore."

"*¡Ay güey!*" Zav stood back up and huffed. "Tell Peggy I need new pants."

Earnie hobbled up to them with a grin on his wrinkly face. "What size? Might have an old pair you can try on."

Luz poked her head past the trailer's opening. "Earnie! Ready to meet a new addition to the farm?"

"What've we got ourselves this time?" He opened the gate to make way, and turned around to get a good view of the creature. "Whoa, this one's got some chompers on it."

Guiding the spinosaurus down and off the ramp, Luz went into guide mode. "Solita here is a spinosaurus, getting its name from the large sail on its back." Keeping a hand on Solita's neck, she patted Earnie on the shoulder while passing him. "Good to see you, Gramps."

"Solita, huh?" He caught sight of the burn marks on the semiaquatic theropod's side. "Now, who would do something like that to the poor thing?"

Passing through the gate, Luz left the spinosaurus, letting it find its own way. "Some kind of electrical prod, I think. Whatever it is...." She crossed her arms, not wanting to admit a certain possibility. "Something tells me Dad's involved with it somehow."

Zav had made his way over to the elderly man. "And something tells me this is no ordinary farm."

"If you're gonna get wrapped up in this, too, you're gonna have to tell the difference between farms and ranches, boy." Earnie chuckled. "Welcome to what your sister and I like to call *Primeval Ranch*."

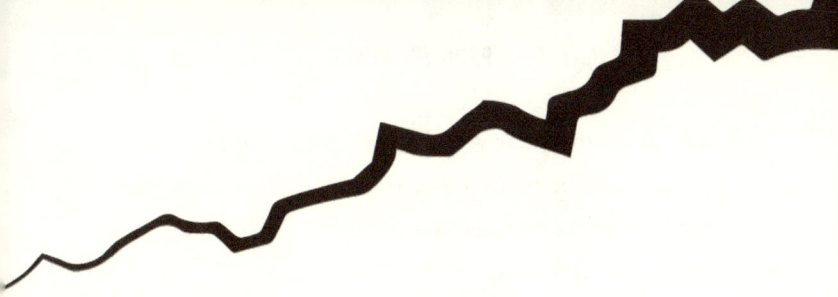

# TEN

**ENTERING AN** old, run-down business in a rough neighborhood, Humberto followed Alvaro back to a makeshift meeting room.

Little had been said between them on the drive in.

When they found others waiting for them, some nods and curious looks were given.

Nodding back and keeping quiet, Humberto passed by a woman banking online with her phone.

She turned slightly, shielding her info from his possibly prying eyes.

At any given moment, day or night, deals were being made. No one really had to worry about their cashflow coming to a standstill.

Humberto didn't think much of her personal business as he sat down in an empty chair.

Alvaro took up an end seat at the temporary meeting table. "El Cazador won't be joining us tonight, but he wanted me to update you all on a…*concerning* issue."

"If it had been my crew, we would have taken them out," one of the lieutenants piped up, full of bravado. "Izan always underestimates and never has enough—"

"Don't talk about my brother like that, Raf," another cartel member growled. "I may never see him again."

A woman snickered from a corner while toying with her combat knife. "All he needed was me as backup."

"Enough!" Alvaro barked, slapping his open palm against the table.

Everyone went silent.

"Word is, SauraCorps is responsible for capturing Izan and his crew." Standing up, Alvaro started pacing. "We used to deal with them back before new ownership took over."

A man sporting a leather jacket spoke up. "Didn't that Arrowsmith guy used to work for them? He was decent business. Whatever happened to him?"

"Sources say his solo operation is no more. Some rumors suggest he was…eaten by his own pet," Alvaro informed the table. "Now, the new head honcho of SauraCorps is trying to undo everything the business had done prior to his takeover."

Humberto added his voice to the conversation. "*Undo?* What does that mean, exactly?"

Crossing his tattooed arms, Alvaro chewed on his bottom lip. "They brought these animals into the present, now they're trying to send them all back. The more they send back, the less cargo we have to move."

The woman in the corner sheathed her knife. "We've

made more money with dinosaurs than we ever did with drugs. Are we going on the offensive?"

"I appreciate your drive, Blanca." Alvaro sighed as he looked up and down the table of his associates. "As long as we stay out of SauraCorps' crosshairs, then we can continue our normal operations."

Wearing a confident grin, Raf picked a piece of food out of his teeth. "And if they get in our way, we'll be more than ready to fight back."

About to suggest a different, non-violent option, Humberto considered his current company and opted to say nothing.

"Hopefully it doesn't come down to a fight." Alvaro grabbed the top rail of the chair he'd sat in. "But if SauraCorps tries to come after any one of us again, El Cazador has instructed us to use any and every force necessary."

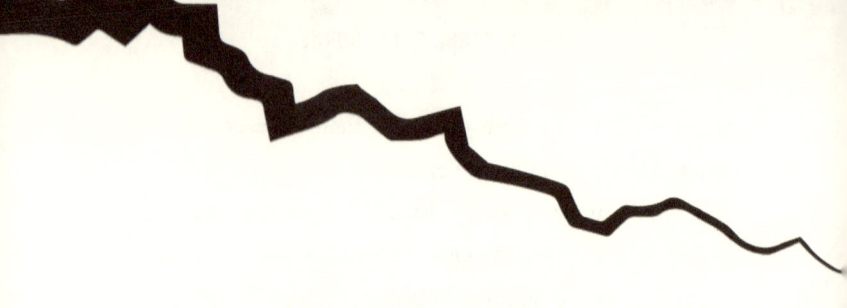

# ELEVEN

**"SAUROPELTA BABIES!"** Lucero squealed as they approached a clutch of five sticking close to their mother. Her voice went an octave lower as she combined words together. "*Ohmurgudnersh,* they're so adorable!"

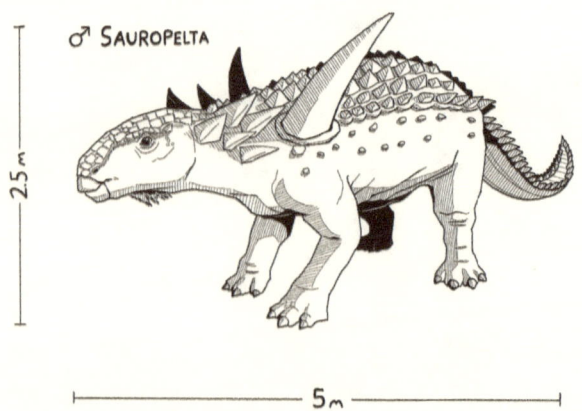

♂ SAUROPELTA
2.5 m
5 m

"Momma Stella's been keeping a close eye on all of 'em." Earnie shuffled over to the parent dinosaur, avoided significant spikes lining its shoulder and neck, and gave her scratches under the chin. "All seem to be healthy lil' spikeys."

Zav kept a twenty-foot distance from the dinosaurs. "Don't tell me all the animals here have names, too."

"'Cept for these youngin's," Earnie responded with delight.

Luz crouched as three of the little dinosaurs bumbled over. "Forget cats, I want more from the dino distribution system."

Grinning at the squealing sauropelta newborns, Zav chuckled. "Gonna name those, too?"

Yawning, Earnie covered his mouth with an arm. "Let's make that a project for tomorrow. Ol' Earnie needs some shuteye soon."

"Might need to wait a few months, actually." Luz picked up one of the sauropelta infants. It squirmed in her arms for a moment before settling in against her for the body heat. "Some lizards, like bearded dragons, can only be identified by three or four months if they're a boy or girl."

Zav smirked. "Do you ever stop being a nerd?"

She nuzzled her nose against the baby dinosaur's. "Better being a nerd than following the herd."

Laughing at the two of them, Earnie's shoulders bounced. "Listening to you two makes me miss my siblings."

Managing a step forward, Zav made his way to his sister. "Dad would be splitting us up by n—"

"Oh frig, *Dad's* trailer!" Luz accidentally squeezed the sauropelta before letting it back down to the ground. "You need to get it back to the house *asap!*"

"Shoot, you're right." Fishing his hand into a pant pocket for his keys, Zav couldn't keep his hand from shaking. "Only thing scarier than a dinosaur is an angry Humberto." About to book it to his truck, he shook the keys in the air before using them to point with. "But when he comes home and finds an empty trailer...."

"*¡Maldita sea!*" Luz waved her arms around, unsure of what to do with her hands. She recalled the spinosaurus wedging its snout through the door as it opened. "What if.... It has to look like something happened to it, some sort of damage."

Earnie pursed his lips. "I've got some sluggos in the shed."

"Sluggos?" Zav cocked his head in confusion.

"Sledgehammers," Earnie clarified, already heading toward his batten boarded shed. "Make it look like the big critter bashed its way out."

On her way to the trailer, Luz patted Zav on the arm. "Go help Earnie, we need to be quick. If Dad's already home...."

The Sanchez kids gave each other troubled stares.

"Dad will kill me if he is, but..." A tremor snuck into Zav's voice. "...something tells me someone else would *actually* kill me."

Not wanting to contemplate the possibility, Luz scrunched her eyebrows together. "Don't think... Don't even talk like that, Zavier."

"Why else do you think he'd be carrying a spinosaurus around?" He stepped closer, bringing their faces inches away from each other. "He's always off on 'jobs,' gets phone calls at all times of the night, and he always deflects when we ask him about any of it."

A teardrop rolled down her cheek. "Just...*stop*, Zav."

Earnie returned, carrying a sledgehammer in each hand. "Whoa now, what's got you all flustered?"

Luz found herself frozen on the spot and unable to speak. If their assumptions turned out to be true of their father, of him working for some cartel organization, the situation would most definitely end up critical.

Zav wrapped an arm around her shoulders, pulling her in close. "Lucero, if we don't go and do this now—"

"Then let's go." She swiped one of the heavy mallets from Earnie before marching off. "Come on, let's destroy this thing before someone destroys our family."

# TWELVE

**ONCE DAMAGE** had been done to the trailer and Zavier drove off, Earnie and Lucero reconvened in his bungalow-style home. Earnie had changed records, and *Till the End of Time* by Dick Haynes sounded from the player's flower petal horn.

Lucero recalled from their first conversation about music that this particular song always reminded him of his late wife. She'd grown to appreciate it as well, though it made her think about her mom.

"So what's this about your dad?" Earnie had finished pouring glasses of water, and brought one over to his adopted granddaughter. "Is he in some sorta trouble?"

About to take a sip, Luz pulled the glass away from her mouth. "I don't, uh… I really hope not."

"Well, if he's been hauling dinosaurs around…" He scratched at the side of his balding head. "…then your brother is right to be afraid."

She gulped down some of the refreshing liquid, hoping it would push down the uncomfortable dryness in her throat. "But he's a good dad." She set the glass down on the kitchen island. "He's always said he would never let anything bad happen to us."

"No doubt about it." He nodded. "And parents always have the best intentions for their children."

"But then why would he even think about joining...."

They gave each other solemn glances.

Neither of them wanted to say the word, as if it would validate everything.

Earnie cleared his throat. "A cartel?"

Though Luz had only been drinking water, her stomach tightened into a sickening knot. "I don't even know what to say to that."

Compassion covered his face. "Sometimes...what we think is helping is actually hurting everyone else around us." He glanced over to his fireplace, where pictures of his family had been placed. "I thought I'd been helping Marilyn keep strong by staying by her side during her last days. Never thought her *days* in the hospital would turn into *months*."

She followed his gaze to the little framed memories. "How did that hurt people?"

He ran his tongue along his bottom teeth. "I'd spent so much time worrying about her that I..." A short inhale preceded a concentrated exhale. "...lost my own self in her last days and pushed everyone else away. I got angry... and resentful, expecting our kids to visit more often as she declined. I kept thinking to myself, 'She's their mother, and they should know better.'" His mouth quaked as he raised the glass to his lips. "At least your father still spends time with you. My kids want nothing to do with me now."

Reaching over, she placed her hand on his. "It's never too late to reach out to them."

Breathing in deeply, he huffed out air to stop himself from getting emotional. "I'm nothing but an ol' stubborn crow to them now."

She snorted at him. "You're not *that* old, Earnie."

"I got bunions almost twice your age," he countered with a half-grin. "And they're not fun-ions, believe me."

"Typical grandpa jokes." Luz laughed at his corny, kid-at-heart nature. "Guess you're ready for some sleep, huh?"

"Yep, need my beauty sleep to wipe away some of these wrinkles." Earnie took a last sip of his water before groaning to get up from the island stool. "Doesn't seem to be working, though."

"I'll stop keeping you up then," she giggled in reply, giving him a pat on the back before heading to the guest room.

She passed by the dining room table, spotting some papers sticking out from a manila envelope. Lettering that resembled something familiar caught her eye. "Earnie? What's all this—"

"Oh, don't mind any of that." He rushed over faster than usual, swishing the documents into the envelope. "It's boring 'old people' stuff."

Picking up on a secretive tone, she decided to not push

it. "If you say so."

Entering the spare bedroom, she slumped onto the bed and placed her phone on the bedside table. As soon as it left her hand, she remembered Daira's texts. Grabbing it again, she opened up to their conversation.

The first message bubble showed:

**Luz, we need to talk.**

Luz rolled her eyes as drowsiness set in.

**Please, Luz, this has been a HUGE misunderstanding.**

Snorting, Luz yawned as she turned over onto her side. *Yeah, sure it is.* Before she could read on, she drifted off into sleepy unconsciousness.

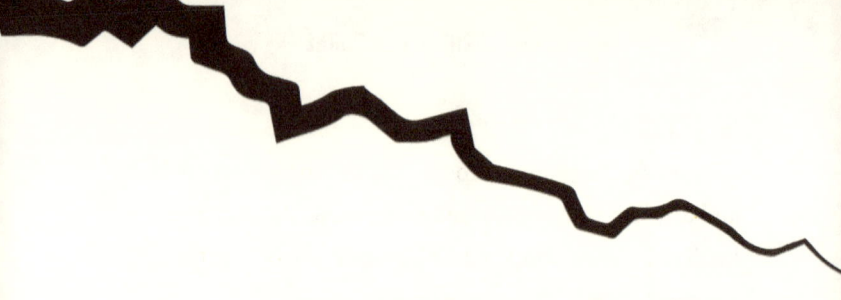

# THIRTEEN

"**CRAP,** crap, *crap!*"

Zavier had maneuvered his pickup truck up onto the grass beside his dad's. Hopping out, he left it running as he bolted for the trailer hitch.

His hands shook as he unhooked the dangling chains. Sweat dripped from his brow. Glancing over his shoulder, he acknowledged no sound or sight of his dad.

*Click-Pop!*

Releasing the coupler from the metal ball, he staggered as the trailer's weight took over.

Zav struggled to keep it balanced, but found it to be too much for him. "*Grrrraaaah*—was easier…with Luz here!"

One shaky footstep took him in the right direction.

His shoes crunched into the gravel as he wrestled for another step.

Five more feet, and he could reattach the trailer to his dad's truck. Every muscle in his being screamed at him as he forced another stomp forward.

Three feet.

Taking quick breaths, he clenched his teeth and willed another agonizing step.

*Bwerrrrp.*

He moved through his own stench.

"*Eeeegh*…. Dang…shrimp…tacos."

Two feet.

"Come…*oooon!*"

Straining his back and arms, Zav engaged everything he had for a final push. Lifting with his legs, he used the momentum to heave the coupler to its destination.

*Ker-chink-click!*

Zavier fell backward, plopping onto the mix of gravel and grass. Letting out a crazed laugh of accomplishment, he laid back the rest of the way. His body thanked him for finally being able to relax.

A distant engine rumbled.

Popping back up, Zav scrambled to hook the chains back into place.

Gazing over to the source of the vehicle sounds, he spotted Alvaro's truck pulling up to a stop sign. He spun on his heels and hustled for the house until a second engine registered in his ears. *My damn truck.*

Alvaro's truck made the turn.

Booking it, Zav could barely feel his legs as he leapt for his keys, twisted the ignition off, and yanked them out. Slamming the driver-side door shut, he turned back and sprinted with the little energy he had left.

Inside Alvaro's truck, both men took double takes as they pulled up.

The trailer door—bashed and broken—laid wide open.

"*¡Hijo de la....*" Humberto exited the vehicle in a fury. "How did… This is…."

"*Santa Madre.*" Alvaro hopped out with a measure of concern, and joined in the inspection. "This was the spino shipment for the Cubans, *sí?*"

"And I plugged the cord in and everything to keep it asleep," Humberto explained, overwhelmed by the level of adrenaline pumping through his body. His feet went on autopilot as he came around the side.

The cord had been removed.

"But who would have…." Humberto put a hand to his mouth as he examined the surrounding neighborhood.

Inside the house, Zavier stood by their back door. He could hear both men through the screen as he regained his breath.

Humberto's sigh turned into a frustrated roar.

Alvaro cracked his knuckles. "Listen, the boss isn't going to like any explanation we try to give him. Without witnesses to what happened here—"

"I'm *dead.*" Humberto cried out, louder than he'd expected to. "I know I'm dead."

Waving a dismissive hand, Alvaro made a contrary groan. "I'll talk to him about—"

"*You will not believe what happened!*"

Both men turned their collective gaze to Zav.

Humberto froze, worried about Alvaro and his son being

in the same space together.

"Earlier, Luz and I were inside, right?" Thankfully, Zav didn't have to act like he was freaked out. "And there was this wicked loud banging from outside."

Suspicious, Alvaro squinted at the boy. "Did you two open—"

"Heck no!" Zav cleared his throat before continuing. "We came out, and the trailer was rocking back and forth like bwam-bam-bwam! And I was all, '*What the heck is thaaaat?*' And Luz was all, '*I don't freaking know!*'"

Humberto glanced around to the neighbors, hoping his son's animated retelling wouldn't get too loud. "Okay, just quiet down a bit, and just—"

"And then there was this big '*Raaaaaah!*' and I was all '*Aaaaaah!*'" Zav made sure to sell the fear with crazed eyes. "And the spinosaurus broke its way out."

"Are you both okay?" Humberto inquired as he came nearer to his boy.

"Luz is fine, I crapped my pants."

Alvaro raised a finger. "How…did you know it was a *spinosaurus?*"

"My sister's a super-nerd."

Humberto gave his son a one-armed hug. "Is she inside?"

"No," Zav leaned into his dad, keeping his head down. "Once the dinosaur ran off, she needed to calm down, so I drove her to Earnie's."

Alvaro looked around the quiet neighborhood. "It couldn't have gotten far without drawing attention. I'll do a drive around and make some calls."

"I should join you. This is my responsibility." Humberto kept his arm around Zav, wanting to go help, but also needing to be with his son.

Already heading for his pickup truck, Alvaro stopped to look back. Seeing the two Sanchez family members being so close made a corner of his mouth twitch into an apologetic smile. "If I need you, I'll call you."

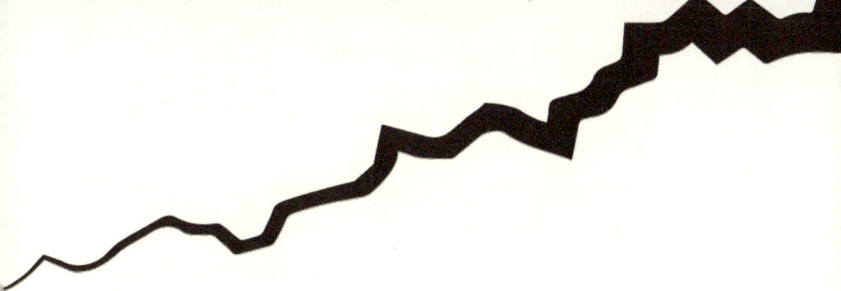

# FOURTEEN

## NUUKSIO NATIONAL PARK, FINLAND

*"AAAAUUUUGGHH!"*

Shocked out of sleep, Landon Halloway sat up while mostly enveloped by his sleeping bag. *Is this a dream?* He'd pitched his tent in a small clearing near one of the park's picturesque lakes. His mind raced as to what could've made one of his friends scream out into the night.

Beside him, his wife yawned and mumbled, "What…was that?"

"I don't know." Wiping his face, Landon reached up for their lantern hanging from the tent's inner peak. "Watch your eyes, Skye."

He flicked it on to full power, illuminating their entire tent.

"Did…someone scream?" Skye guessed as she rolled over.

Landon slipped a shirt on as he grabbed a flashlight. "I'm

gonna go check it out."

"Remember, Finland has bears and wolves, so be careful."

He gulped. "Yeah, *thanks* for that reminder."

Unzipping the front flap, he exited the confines of their small shelter and took a couple staggering steps into the Finnish wilderness.

They'd planned a rugged camping trip along with three other couples. Only two days in, the group had already had a relatively pleasant encounter with a curious herd of long-necked dinosaurs.

As for nocturnal wildlife—modern-day or prehistoric—they hadn't come across any.

Directing his flashlight around the small clearing to his friends, he discovered all three of their tents still standing.

*Crick-crack-crick-crack-crick-crack.*

Spinning around to locate the source of the odd sound, he tripped over one of the firepit rocks. He barely caught himself from landing directly in the glowing ashes and swore under his breath.

"Landon?" Skye poked her head through the tent door. "Oh jeez, babe, are you okay?"

"I'm fine, just need to watch where I'm go—"

"*Noooo—aaaaaauugh!*"

Swinging the flashlight's beam to the left, Landon pinpointed the yell. "That's the Vale's tent."

*Hissssssssssss!*

*Snip-snap-whump!*

Rods broke haphazardly as the polyester material enfolded and muffled more screams from their friends.

Retreating into their own tent, Skye called out, "What's happening out there?"

"I don't...." Landon froze, afraid of what lurked among the foliage. "Something is attacking—"

"No, no, *no!*" Off to the right, another of their buddies crawled halfway out of his tent. "Landon! Landon, help m—*aaaahhhh!*"

Already bolting toward him, Landon hollered, "Carmelo, hold on!"

Dragged back into his tent, Carmelo dug his fingers into the grass and yelled out, "Just get out of—"

Silence.

Only rips and cracks came from Carmelo's tent.

Immediately after, the third tent flipped over, sending the Minshall family tumbling as a creature made its way inside.

Landon caught the tail end of the animal's hide slightly glisten in the moonlight. "What in the actual...."

*Crick-crack-crick-crack.*

Another creature skulked nearby.

Only one thing entered his mind. *Skye.*

Sprinting back, he dove back into his tent and began shoving things into one of their duffle bags. "Skye, we have to leave *now.*"

Skye matched his level of frenzy and began doing the same. "Do you even know what's out there?"

"No idea, but whatever it is..." Landon placed a hand on her shoulder. "...they've taken out everyone else."

Tears burst from her eyes. "Oh my God."

*Crick-crack-crick-crack.*

*Hissssss!*

As soon as the strange sound met their ears, both of them went quiet.

Chin trembling, Skye whispered, "What the heck is—"

"*Just...*" Landon whispered with intensity. "...*be... quiet.*" Slowly, he reached up and lowered the lamp's brightness.

*Crick-crack-crick-crack.*

A creature brushed up against the material on Skye's side.

Whimpering, she backed up into her husband. "What the frig—"

Landon cupped a hand over his wife's mouth.

Something bumped into the back of their tent.

*Hisssssss!*

Undeterred, it began slipping underneath, making the floor material ripple.

"Oh my *Go-ho-hod!*" Skye shoved Landon's hand off of her.

They swished their sleeping bags around their small shelter. Failing to get as far away from it as possible, for a moment, their attention turned from the intruding animal to them clinging to each other.

He stared into her eyes. "Skye, if we don't make—"

"Landon..." With tears in her eyes, she placed a hand on his cheek. "...I love you."

*RIIIIIIIIIIIIIIP!*

*Crick-crack-crick-crack.*

A giant millipede poked its armored head through a hole in the tent floor.

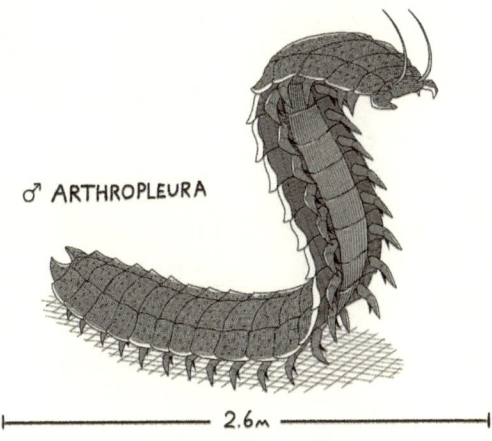

♂ ARTHROPLEURA

|— 2.6ᴍ —|

Its grotesque legs flexed and jittered as its mandibles twitched.

Landon kicked at it as hard as he could as Skye shrieked.

The oversized and starving arthropleura arched itself within the confines of the tent, making the lamp sway back and forth as it lunged forward.

*HISSSSSSSS!*

The Halloways' screams echoed throughout the clearing.

At dawn, an off-roading SUV parked on the grass.

Hopping out of the passenger seat, a man surveyed the campsite.

Decimated.

Four giant millipedes still feasted.

The Finnish driver took one look at the sickening scene and immediately thrust his door open to empty his stomach.

"Gorgeous creatures, aren't they?" After an impressed whistle, the passenger pulled out his cellphone to take pictures and send some texts. "Looks like that tip from the cartel has definitely paid off."

After wiping his mouth, the driver spit out the residue. "And you want to take these bugs with you?"

"Of course." Glancing back to him, the man grinned. "They'll make an excellent addition to my *collection*."

# FIFTEEN

**"LANDED,** famished, and on my way." Zoey marched past people waiting around the airline carousels for their luggage. With a carry-on bouncing against her left side, she held her cellphone in her right hand. "Remind me again of who I'm looking for?"

"His name is Evander, I think he's already waiting for you." On the other end of the line, Sebastian pulled some files together. "Sending you a headshot now."

"Evander, huh?" She made a turn and went down some stairs. "Sounds sexy."

"He's ex-military."

Sebastian's message made the phone buzz against her ear.

Zoey swung the screen in front of her to open the image. "Dark brown hair, broody chocolate eyes, gorgeous dark skin tone, fine jawline—Seb, did you pull this guy out of a dark romance book?"

"Rock Springs, Wyoming, actually."

Strolling through an open set of double doors, she'd finally surpassed the arrivals hall of the Corpus Christi International Airport. "Talk to you soon, gotta tame the hangry beast a.k.a. my stomach." Hanging up, she hurried over to the in-airport restaurant. She claimed one of the stools at the bar and kept her carry-on bag close by her feet.

"What would you like?" asked the bartender.

"Know how to make a Diamondback?"

The woman gave a puzzled stare. "I'll…look it up."

After taking one glance at the food menu, Zoey raised a finger. "And a Coastal Bend Burger with a fried egg—oh, and sweet potato fries, please and thanks. I'm jonesing for some brioche."

A few moments later, her drink arrived.

She picked it up and zoned in on the brandied cherry. "Oooh, come to meeee, *babyyyy*—"

"Hope you don't mind *turbulence,* honey, 'cause you got my heart *racing,*" an inebriated man blurted out as he took up the seat next to her.

Finishing her sip, Zoey didn't spare a glance at him. "Wow, a flying pun in an airport, how original."

The drunk got the attention of the bartender. "Put her drink…on my-my tab." He turned back to Zoey and slurred as he continued. "Hope you don't mind *ssssoaring,* becaushe our connection is *heights*—er, I mean, uh—"

"How about boarding a flight back to whatever hole you crawled out of, mkay, bye." She still didn't give him an ounce of eye contact. Turning her back to him, she took a satisfactory sip from her cocktail.

"Listen, honey." Undeterred, the man placed a hand on her side. "Maybe if you smiled more and loosened up a bit—"

Zoey's eyes flared open.

Evander checked his watch. *She should be here by now.*

Letting his handwritten "Beaumont" sign fall to his side, he picked up on the crackle of a security guard's walkie-talkie.

"May need backup at the restaurant." The guard already started heading toward the disturbance. "Altercation between a young brunette and a drunk guy."

Curious, Evander rolled his shoulders to loosen up as he followed along. *Altercation?*

Making his way through a security door, the guard realized he'd been tailed. "Excuse me, sir, you can't come through—"

"F.B.I." Evander revealed a badge. "Let me help." Allowed through and coming out the other side, it didn't take long for him to zone in on the disturbance.

A drunk man yelled out, "Calm down, you—*aaaaaaugh!*" Flailing out the front of the restaurant, his backside hit the hard floor first. "Goddammit, woman!"

Zoey leapt onto the man, lodging her knee into his groin as she walloped him with a left fist. "What's the matter, huh? Gonna tell me I'm not like other girls?" Her right hook met his temple. "Or that I'm on my period?"

Evander gave his soon-to-be mission partner an impressed look as he rushed over.

"You're insane," the drunk cried out. "Get the heck off—"

"That's enough." Grabbing Zoey's shoulders, Evander hauled her back. "Come on, Beaumont, he ain't worth it."

Trying to wriggle free, Zoey scoffed. "That's right, because he's a disgusting piece of...." She glanced at the strong hands, then turned to get a better look. "Evander, right?"

He grunted in amusement. "Been waiting for you."

"Yeah, well, had to grab a burger first."

"Was feeding him fists a side option?"

"Sweet potato fries, actually." She straightened her light blue jacket and shirt. "Defending womankind was the dessert."

Evander raised an eyebrow, trying to figure her out. Taking into consideration the number of security guards that had convened around them, he showed his F.B.I. badge once more. "She's with me, I'll take her off your hands."

Bemused, Zoey squinted at him. "Wait, you're *F.B.I.?* Seb didn't—"

"How about we get that burger *to go,* huh?" Evander avoided the question by grabbing her arm and gently leading her away from the crowd. "Plus, you owe me fries for this."

Outside of the airport, Zoey followed Evander to his parked vehicle. "Thanks for bailing me out back there, but I had it handled."

He gave an unimpressed glance while unlocking the doors. "*Definitely* had it handled."

She smirked. "Sarcasm *definitely* detected."

Getting in the driver's seat, he stared straight ahead. "That a bad thing?"

"We won't need a translator." Holding her takeout in her right hand, she let the strap of her carry-on slip off her left shoulder. Opening the rear door, she swung it inside, then reached for the front passenger handle. "At least you have some sense of hum—"

"Nu-uh, don't even think about getting burger juice on Betty's seat," he warned with an adamant stare while holding out a halting hand. "This is a Mercedes-Benz E-fifty-five AMG and it will not be—"

"Betty—what now?" She had already placed a foot inside. "You're seriously one of those guys that names his car?"

He growled as he wagged a pointed finger. "Finish it outside."

"Dude, they gave me napkins."

"*Outside.*"

Removing her foot from the car, she placed the takeout package on top of the car. "Great, Seb's got me paired with a control fre—"

"Remove the food from the roof," he added, maintaining his annoyed tone. "Just got this waxed on Wednesday."

Bringing her face to the passenger window, she scowled at him. "Oh, so you're gonna sit in your car while I pop a squat…on the curb?"

"Whatever saves my detailed seats," he responded with a

triumphant grin. "Now hurry it up, gotta get debriefed by Seb soon."

She pulled a sweet potato waffle fry from the takeout container. "Let me in and I'll actually give you some fries."

With displeasure in his eyes, he looked over and revealed a sliver of a smirk. "One crumb or grease drop, and you'll be in a world of pain."

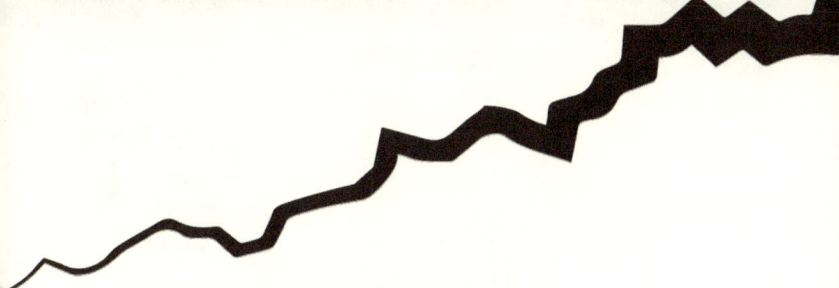

# SIXTEEN

**MORNING TEA** in hand, Lucero opened the back door of Earnie's place. It led to a roof-covered deck, which gave the perfect view of the barn and open space.

Being fairly close to Big Bend National Park, the lush terrain provided the perfect environment for the prehistoric and present creatures around.

As a sip of the warm drink trickled down her throat, she grinned as a pair of glyptodons scuttled up to the wooden deck stairs.

One of the fluffy white barn cats sat on the top of one, enjoying the little voyage.

Luz disembarked the deck and set down her mug. "Good morning, Georgie and Gladys. And Libby, are you getting a free ride?"

Excited to see their human friend again, the two-ton glyptodons snorted and made guttural squeals like a bear mixed with a pig.

♀ GLYPTODON

1.7 m

3.3 m

Their noises didn't even concern Libby as she rolled over and stretched out over Georgie's warm shell.

Giving the prehistoric armadillos gentle taps on the armored caps of their heads, Luz brought her hands under their chins for some scratches. "Still keeping with the morning routine, huh?" She pulled bits of straw from their furry faces, and made sure to scritch behind their ears. "Other than the hay bales, are we keeping out of trouble around here?"

In response to the scratches, both glyptodons lowered their heads and rocked their armadillo-like shells back and forth.

Libby finally took offense, sliding down and off the glyptodon.

Further away, a megatherium—which Luz had based her latest sketch on—lumbered along, checking a little berry bush for ripe ones.

She giggled at the giant ground sloth. "Morning, the magnificent Maya!"

"Don't be eatin' all my berries, now, Maya." Earnie

stepped out into the morning sun. "Ah, the glyptos are making their rounds, huh?"

"*Glip-toe-dons*," Luz corrected with a giggle in her voice. "Do I have to give you phonetic lessons again?"

"Nicknames work for me," he countered while readjusting one of the straps to his overalls. "Georgie's front claws almost slashed my leg the other day when I brought 'em food."

"Yet another reminder to always respect any creature and what they can do." Luz gave them pats on their heads and grabbed her tea. "*Ice Age* did not do glyptodons justice."

"What's that, now?"

"It's a classic animated movie."

"Everything's a classic to me, darlin'."

She chuckled at his subtle self-deprecation. "You're an oldie but a goodie."

He laughed before gulping his coffee. "How 'bout we stop talking about my age and get you all set up to ride."

As they headed for the barn, Luz brimmed with anticipation. "Did the saddle designer ask any questions about the dimensions?"

"Quite a few, actually." Earnie opened the door for her, then headed in behind her. "Told 'em I had a new idea for a tree swing, but wanted something fancier than a flimsy ol' tire."

Once inside the barn, Luz placed both hands around her mouth, drew in a big breath, and hollered, "*Teeeeeeeeeeeess!*"

Her voice echoed throughout the structure, making it even louder.

"*Heeeere,* girl." She shouted, and mustered more air into her lungs. "Come *oooon*, Tess!"

*THUD-BOOM!*

Earnie nodded. "Must've still been sleeping outside."

*RRRROOOOOOUUUUUUHH!*

Over at the large open doorway, the summoned dinosaur poked its large head through. Tess the tarbosaurus delivered a low grumble as she ducked to enter the barn halfway.

3.5 m

♀ TARBOSAURUS

12 m

Also known as a Mongolian tyrannosaurus rex, Tess swung her proportionally bigger head toward the girl to give her a big friendly sniff. Her little arms hung down as she flexed her reptilian fingers.

Unafraid, Luz placed a flat palm against the tip of Tess's nose. Now connected by touch, she slowly slid her hand up and above the top eye ridge. "Ready for today, Tess? We got you a present, hopefully you like it."

"It'll most likely take both of us to get it on her," Earnie piped up, already struggling with the heavier-than-usual saddle as he shimmied it onto a wheelbarrow.

Luz made clicking noises with her mouth in tandem with

a hand placed against Tess's chin. It had been over a week since she'd spent time at Earnie's, and she hoped the trained signal would still work. "Curtsy, Tess. *Curtsy.*"

Bending at the knees, the five-ton tarbosaurus lowered herself to the ground.

"Atta girl." Earnie finished wheeling the saddle over. "The front straps have a hackamore bridle, figured it would help us keep our hands and digits. Make sure none of that gets too tight for her when it's on, Luz."

She grabbed the front of the contraption as Earnie lifted the back. It took under half a minute to maneuver it on, then they focused on strap positions.

He glanced over at the teenage girl at one point and gave her a proud smile. As he snaked two more thick fastenings under Tess's belly, his smile turned into a pensive purse of the lips. "You know, after our little talk last night, I couldn't help but ask myself something I should be asking you."

She attached the open muzzle which enabled Tess to still open her mouth, and made it comfortable for the dinosaur. "Don't tell me, you're going to ask it now, right?"

He raised an eyebrow at her along with a wry smirk. "Don't get smart with me, girl." Getting the final strap in place, he came around and checked everything over. "Now, you know I love having you here helping me out with all these critters. But have you ever thought about what you'll do with your life beyond all this?"

With her hand still attached to the snug collar, Luz let her arm relax and hang. "You mean like, a job?" She let her fingers run along Tess's scaley back as she advanced toward the saddle. "I love working here, and I told you I don't need your money. Dad's job is—"

"That's not...." He rubbed the side of his face. "What I mean is, *this*." He spread his arms out and swayed with purpose. "All of this can't, and most likely won't, last forever. Heck, I probably don't have many years left in me, and—"

"I'm fifteen," she retorted, already climbing up onto Tess. "Pretty sure I've got a couple of years until I start thinking more seriously about life."

Earnie helped her up using his palm against her shoe, then wiped his hand on his overalls. "True, and I'm always an advocate for kids staying kids as long as possible, and don't forget to ride the—"

"Ride the gravy train as long as I can," she finished alongside him in a sing-song manner. Gazing down to Earnie from her perched position on the tarbosaurus, she switched focus to her hands fidgeting with the reins. "What are you trying to say, Earnie?"

With one hand on his hip, he rubbed the back of his neck with the other. "Luz, my door is *always* open to you, no matter what, when, or why."

Luz gave him an endearing smile. "I know."

"Just..." He gave her a solemn stare. "...you need to be prepared for when it's *not my door* anymore."

Her eyes welled up, but she wiped them with the back of her hand before they got worse. "Um... I'm going to take Tess for a spin." Creating clicking noises with her mouth again, she patted the dinosaur on its side. "Let's go on an adventure, Tess."

# SEVENTEEN

**AFTER PULLING** into a local hotel, Evander and Zoey headed inside. Bags in hand, they needed to check in before a clandestine chat with Sebastian.

Evander marched up to the hotel front office and met with a young man. "Two rooms, queen beds, please."

"Oooh, sorry, bro." The clerk tapped on his keyboard. "Unfortunately, we've only got one room left with a king."

Hearing the word "bro" made Evander's mouth twitch in disgust.

Placing her hands on the counter's edge, Zoey leaned in. "You serious? How is it that busy right now?"

"Little league baseball tournament," the clerk answered simply. "America's favorite sport, am I right, bro?"

Meanwhile, Zoey's phone buzzed. Checking the message from the lock screen, she noted Sebastian's text.

**Ready to talk when you are, but I've got a half-**

**hour window.**

"Listen, *bro*." Evander balled his hands into fists, keeping them at his sides. "One room doesn't quite work with our situation here. Kids are small and compact, I'm sure you can fit more into—"

"We'll take it, bro." Zoey pulled out her wallet and credit card. "Two nights for now."

Evander shot her a surprised glare. "What? Really? You're okay with this—with *us?*"

"This is a job." She paid for the room and shoved her wallet back in her duffle bag. "I'm sure we can both keep it professional, right, *Captain America?*"

About to make a negative remark, Evander didn't mind the pop culture reference. "Fine."

Accepting the room keys from the young clerk, Zoey started for the elevator. "Seb's ready to talk to us *now.*"

Up and settled in their room, Zoey flopped onto the king bed. "At least the pillows are comfy. Bed's not bad either."

Evander unzipped his bag and pulled out a laptop. "Enjoy it, I'll be taking the chair."

"You're damn right you're taking the chair."

He uttered an indifferent grumble. "I've slept in much worse conditions."

As she sat up on the bed with her legs outstretched, she tucked a pillow into her side for extra comfort. "Seb said you're ex-military. But you still look fairly young for the word 'ex' to be mentioned."

Focused on setting up the video call, Evander didn't reply.

Zoey studied the stoic look on his face. "If we're going to spend the night and have this mission-baby together—"

"*Don't* say 'mission-baby.'"

She smirked at the loathing in his tone. "Maybe we could actually talk about ourselves. You know, *actually* get to know each other a bit."

A couple of finger taps later, Evander had connected to the encrypted chat.

Sebastian popped up on the screen and wore a warm smile. "Good almost-noon, guys. Sorry to try and rush through this, I've got a family thing to get to."

"No worries, Seb-orino," Zoey scootched closer to the edge of the bed. "Z-Team reporting for duty."

Sitting in the chair he'd claimed to sleep in, Evander let one of his eyes twitch. "Side question, where'd you find this one?"

Sebastian chuckled when Evander pointed at his new partner. "She's a *unique* one, isn't she?"

"Don't you guys know unique makes the world go 'round?" Zoey refuted with a grin. "Now who or what's our target here?"

"Right, down to business." Sebastian nodded, getting files ready to show on the screen. "Two years ago, when we realized time rifts were becoming more unpredictable, Xing and his scientists supplied inverted space-time energy bombs to close the rifts." When he paused, he expanded a window of a holographic globe with indicator dots and shared it with the others. His head shrank down into a smaller frame. "At the Utah SauraCorps base, I had our scientists keep track of every instance of rift energy, whether big or small. When Felicia destroyed the Utah rift with Xing's bomb, we didn't realize how many rifts would blip into existence in aftershock. Some stayed open for seconds, some minutes, others at least an hour, and so on."

Evander leaned in, noting some of the locations. "How many rifts have there been?"

Sebastian opened his mouth, but needed an extra second to find the right words. "Quite a few shown here are rifts. Other instances are.... Let's just say I met *someone* who explained that a gemstone called *Gallaxitium* is essentially what can harness and control space-time."

"*Wait-whoa-wait....*" Zoey's jaw dropped. "There are space-time gemstones embedded in the earth and *no one's* talking about it?"

"They're extremely rare." Sebastian included in his explanation. "And can you imagine if everyone *was* talking about it?"

"World-ending chaos. Fair point. As you were."

After a chuckle, Sebastian continued. "And thanks to this *shall-not-be-named* individual because it's *classified,* their assistance helped me utilize Project Pinpoint to find all rifts that ever opened in the past."

Evander caught on. "So we're checking out past rift opening points?"

"Exactly, Ev." Sebastian clicked on a couple more files and

shared them. "One of our sources supplied intel on another faction of the cartel you helped bust yesterday." A man's headshot came up. "Alvaro Balderas, a lieutenant of—"

"Sorry, did you say Banderas?" Zoey crouched closer to the laptop. "Any relation to—"

"*Bal*-deras, Zo. No Antonio relation." Sebastian shook his head with a smirk. "Alvaro's a lieutenant for a cartel led by an El Cazador."

"El Cazador, huh?" Zoey put on her best Spanish accent. "Would you say he has a...*plethora*...of dinosaurs?"

Sebastian made a slight grin at her *The Three Amigos* movie reference and cleared his throat. "The informant also gave a location on his favorite restaurant haunt." Again, a picture presented itself. "Definitely proceed with caution on this one. Obviously, if we can get more information on their operations, then we can save more time-displaced animals."

"Consider it done." Evander saluted his boss with full confidence. "We'll stake out the restaurant tonight."

Zoey placed a hand to her stomach. "Speaking of stakeouts, I could go for some steak, a little horseradish on the side, oh and a baked—"

"Sorry, guys, I gotta run." Sebastian smiled at his newly formed team. "Be safe out there. Oh, and Zo?"

"Yeah, Seb?"

"Don't have too much fun, all right?"

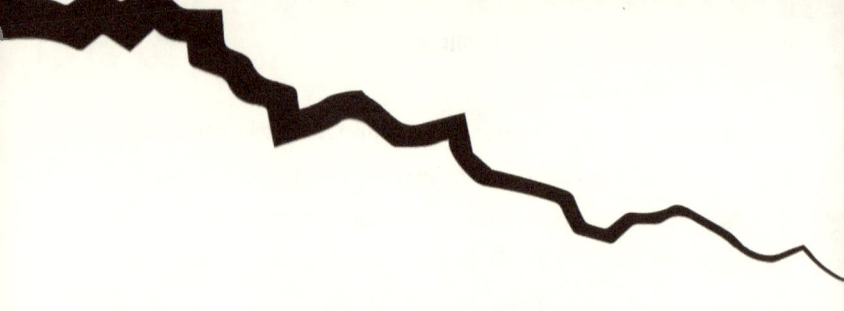

# EIGHTEEN

**FRESH AIR** with hints of wild sage filled Lucero's lungs. Riding Tess the tarbosaurus gave her an even higher vantage point of the gorgeous terrain.

Craggy mountains off in the distance gave a sense of wonder and awe. Multiple shades of green brush and wildflowers, mixed with orange and deep reds in the dirt and rocks. Wide open blue sky made the western paradise even more perfect.

With *Live a Little* by Chaz Cardigan starting to play through her phone's speakers, Luz tightened her grip on the reins. "Well, Tess, let's see what you can do."

A sharp whistle flew out of her mouth as she snapped the reins.

Tess's lumbering strut picked up.

The indie song came to the energizing bridge.

Every thundering step of the tarbosaurus made the surrounding foliage shake.

"Yeah!" Luz crouched while keeping her legs tucked horizontal. "Go, go, *go!*"

Having moderate control over a dinosaur gave her an indescribable thrill. Every flex of Tess's muscles carried up to the saddle, which added to the buzz already flowing through Luz.

Finding their collective rhythm, Luz settled in to the sway of Tess's gallop.

Though no trail snaked along in front of them, Tess followed her instincts. Rabbits scampered off and birds took flight as the dinosaur maintained a ten-mile-an-hour sprint.

Adding tension to the right, Luz directed her prehistoric steed. "How about this way?"

Obliging, Tess yielded to her rider's direction.

Up ahead, a small herd of minmis munched on the plant life.

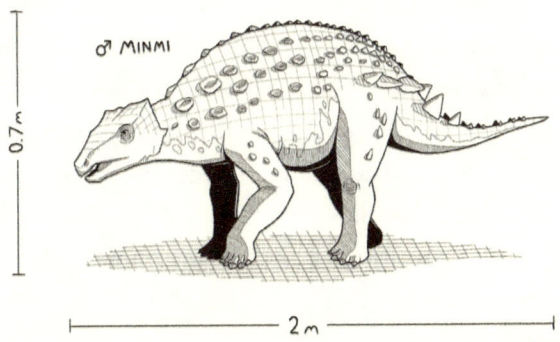

"Watch those guys!" Luz pulled on the left rein, hoping to avoid the family of dinosaurs.

*AAAAAARROOOOOOUUUWNK!*

A single minmi sounded an alarming honk.

The rest of the dark-green, armored dinosaurs scattered, creating more moving obstacles.

"No! Crap!" Luz kept her eyes wide open, even though dust had floated up into the air. As adrenaline pumped throughout her entire body, she fought to stay calm and upright. "Turn, turn, *turn!*"

Tess's left foot grazed the side of a minmi, knocking it off balance.

Another minmi bumped into Tess's right leg.

Getting jostled, Luz's left leg slipped and she lost positioning on the saddle. Dangling against Tess's side, she bounced against the dinosaur's hard, scaley hide. Reins still wrapped around her hand, she engaged her upper body and held on tight.

The tarbosaurus continued to barrel through the area. Having made it out of the minmi's grazing spot, Tess hadn't slowed down.

Wrestling to regain control, Luz screamed as she exerted everything she had to haul herself back up. "Jeez...." Getting her legs back into position, she let her arms relax slightly. "Okay, saddle definitely needs a tweak, and you, Tess, need more training."

As they approached a small lake on Earnie's property, Luz increased tension on the left rein. "*Whoa,* Tess. Slow, *sloooow.*"

Every step Tess took gradually lessened in speed. Coming to a full stop a few feet from the water's edge, she swung her head to-and-fro to take in the watering hole.

"Need to stop for a drink?" Luz tapped Tess on the sides with both hands, swung her legs around, and pointed herself toward Tess's tail. "Now to channel my inner Fred Flinstone." She shimmied over the back of the saddle and began sliding down. Her feet hit the ground, staggered forward a few steps, then maintained some balance. "Huh, worked better than I thought."

Pulling out her phone to see what time it was, she discovered a text from Zavier:

**We need to talk about last night.**

Only one bar of cell reception came in.

A few steps away from the lake, she watched as two more bars graced her phone. She dialed for her brother. "Zav, what's up?"

He kept a somewhat calm voice. "Oh, you know, other than Dad getting into deep crap with a cartel and discovering that you and Earnie are running a little dinosaur farm, everything's absolutely peachy."

Panic made Luz's throat close for a moment. "Our plan with the trailer *didn't* work?"

"I'm hoping the guy that dropped Dad off took the bait," Zav answered with a hint of doubt. "He took off thinking he'd find the spinosaurus somewhere close by. But honestly, I don't know how long they'll be searching for until they suspect something might be up."

She took the phone away from her ear as her heart rate increased for a different reason than trying to control a charging dinosaur. She leaned against one of Tess's legs, who had lowered her head for a drink. "How's Dad?"

"Stressed—oh, hold on, he wants to talk to you."

Concerned about the dinosaurs around her, Luz winced. "Not sure if now is a great time to talk to—"

"Luz, *mija,* how are things at Earnie's?" Humberto spoke with an audible smile. "Have you finished your riding lessons for today?"

"Um, yeah, I actually just took one of the horses out to—"

*ROOOOUUUUUUUUUUUUUH!*

Tess spilled water from her mouth while turning her head to look at the girl.

Humberto didn't say anything for a couple of seconds. "What…was *that?*"

"Uh, it was…." Struggling to come up with a lie, Luz placed a hand on her forehead. "We are…watching a whale documentary. Earnie's old, right? He needs the volume way up."

Again, Humberto took a moment to reply. "A whale documentary?"

"He's a nature fanatic."

"Okay, well, I was going to say that *something happened,* and my delivery was canceled. Now I have a little time on my hands," he explained with increasing excitement. "I was hoping Zav and I could come down and see you ride."

"No!" Luz shouted louder than intended. "I mean—"

"No? Why not?"

"Because…." Luz paused, then picked up on noises coming from all around. "I just—"

*HAAWOOOOOONK! HWONK! HWONK!*

Peggy the parasaurolophus and two of her fellow species stepped into the lake for an afternoon dip, all of them honking with delight.

"It's um—"

*AARROOOOUUWNK!*

"—frig sakes."

The family of minmi from earlier also approached the water for a collective drink.

"What's all that noise?" Utterly confused, Humberto clicked a button on the phone. "That doesn't sound like whales."

Luz realized her dad had requested to switch the conversation to their cameras. "Oh, sorry, Dad, but I don't think—"

"Luz, is something wrong?"

"All good, just have to go help Earnie with something, bye!" Luz hung up just before a number of prehistoric creatures formed a haphazard chorus from their voices. Her chest heaved up and down as her nerves took over. "*Dios mío,* can you all work on your timing, please?"

Tess grumbled, nudging her snout against the anxious human's back.

"I know, I know." Luz took the dinosaur's touch as its way of comforting her. "You're all allowed to make noise." She patted Tess on the cheek and gave her a little scratch. "Let's head on back, and let's take it easy this time."

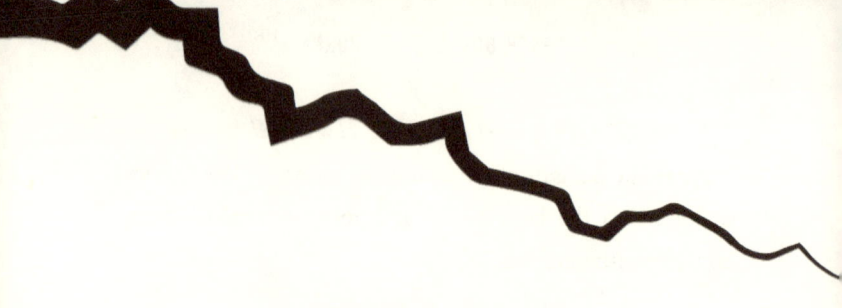

# NINETEEN

**"AND IN** other news, Saura-Portal, the bestselling book by Kamren Eckhardt is currently in development at Universal Studios," a radio host announced. "Sources say no casting has been confirmed, but fans are calling for Spielberg to direct."

"Wow, they're actually going ahead with it." Zoey reclined in the passenger seat as they drove along a country road. "Did you ever read it?"

Evander kept his eyes on the asphalt. "Nope."

"Doesn't surprise me." She glanced over at him before rolling her eyes back to the window. "You're probably one of those people that say audiobooks aren't real books."

"They're books."

She gave him a double take. "Wait, really?"

He waved one of his hands around for emphasis. "Words make a book. Someone reads said book. Still a book."

She gave him a surprised smile. "Hold up, I do believe

we've agreed on something."

He made a casual grunt.

Taking that as a cue to move on, Zo tapped a finger on the glass beside her. "Anyway, I was going to say, it's crazy how that Kam kid turned a real-life experience into a bestseller. He did take some liberties, making Seb a blonde and changing his name to Sterling."

Ev chuckled. "Sterling."

"Also heard he's writing a seq—*whoa!*"

Slamming on the brakes, Ev checked over a list of coordinates they'd been given. "According to this, multiple rifts opened just up that direction."

Right away, she detected glaring deterrents. "And a locked gate with multiple 'No Trespassing' signs is essentially saying, '*You shall not pass.*'"

After putting his car in park, he retrieved his cellphone from his brown leather jacket's inner pocket. "Can't see the house from here, must be a long driveway. I'll make a call and see if I can get the owner's—"

*Slam!*

"—number." Alarmed by Zo leaving, he pushed the button to roll down the window. "Beaumont, where do you think you're going?"

Already a few feet from the typical farmland access gate, she brought a hand over her eyes to block out the sun. "We should go in."

Irritated, he also exited the vehicle. "Things might go *easier* if we do things *by the book.*"

"Boy scout, huh?" Standing at the fence, she rested her

hands on her hips. "Got any binoculars along with your personal achievement badges?"

His upper lip twitched. "Why?"

"Well, if I'm not mistaken…" She strained her eyes a bit more. "…I'm pretty sure there's a few austroraptors out there to the right of the barn. They're darting around like crazy. Plus…yep, that's a megatherium way off to the left. Can barely see it."

Ev pulled binoculars from his trunk. "Some *what-*raptors?"

"*Austro*raptors," she repeated, keeping her sights honed in on them. "Slender raptors with a longer-than-usual snout. Fossils were originally found in Argentina. And then the megatherium, that's like a giant prehistoric version of a sloth."

♂ AUSTRORAPTOR

1.8 m

4.8 m

Closing the trunk, he picked up on a hint of contentment. "Seem to know a fair bit."

Zoey flinched, then immediately forced her grimace into a fleeting grin. "Someone I…*used to* be close to taught me a lot."

Coming over, he placed the army-grade binoculars over his eyes. He scanned some of the landscape in the direction she'd been surveying until the dinosaurs came into view. "Huh, targets spotted."

She wore a mischievous grin. "So, we're going *in,* right?"

He lowered the optical instrument, letting it sway as he dialed a number on his cellphone. *"We* are going to collect intel on the homeowner first."

"There's no *time* for that," she retorted while placing her hands on the top rung of the wooden fence, eager to head inside. "This is our mission; this is *our time* to move."

"And we will operate it the *right way.* "Ev heard the contact connect on the other end and spoke up. "This is Evander Evers requesting contact information for a rural—"

*Thump!*

Zoey had jumped the fence.

Agitated, he pulled the phone further away from his mouth to shout, "Hey! You're breaking the law, and I'm *ordering* you to get back here, *now!"*

Strutting down the gravel driveway, she turned around to holler back, "Don't worry, Ev, I've got a plan."

"Zoey!"

"It's a cunning plan."

*"Zoey!"*

# TWENTY

**TENDING TO** his lunchtime sandwich, Earnie slathered some mustard onto a slice of sourdough bread. The kitchen situated at the front of the house close to the door provided a great vantage point for observing activity on the farm. Picking up a tomato, he glanced out a row of windows while washing it at the sink.

One of his quick glances morphed into a confused stare.

An unfamiliar woman jogged up the driveway.

He set the red fruit down on the counter and grumbled as he headed for a cabinet. "Better be prepared for anything."

Reaching the front deck steps, Zoey studied the windows for movement. Standing at the door, she continued checking around her as her hand neared the screen door.

*Knock-knock-kno—*

"Something tells me you're either stupid or blind." Earnie had pulled the main door open, and aimed his rifle at the uninvited intruder. "Or *both*."

Zo took a step back. "Sorry to bother you, sir, honest. It's just that—"

"*Beaumont!*" Evander ran up to the steps with rage in his eyes as he came to her side. "This is not—"

"My...*boyfriend's* car broke down," she managed to think up, keeping an eye on the weapon being pointed at her. "We hate to be a bother, but could we use your phone?"

About to object, Evander noticed the rifle.

Earnie inspected each of them, checking their body language and assessing their facial expressions. "Neither of you should be here."

"We saw the signs, really, we did." Zo kept up her charade. "But Ev here, his phone is dead and mine's been busted for weeks." She put on her best smile. "We'd both really appreciate it if we could use your—"

*Buzzzz. Buzzzz.*

Everyone heard Ev's phone come to life.

Zoey threw her head back. "Dammit."

*BLA-KOOOOOOW!*

Ev and Zo split as the blast from the rifle blew a hole in the screen.

After staggering back a half-step, Earnie slammed his hand into the tattered door and marched out onto the deck. "Now I *know* you're stupid for thinking I'm dumb."

Unholstering his gun, Ev stumbled into a crouched position. "Mr. Pardy, we mean you *no harm.* Put the weapon down, and we can talk—"

"I'll be putting Roxie down when either of y'all tells me what's *really* going on here," Earnie shouted back.

Rolling onto her side, Zo muttered, "Great, I'm surrounded by men who name their belongings."

"Easy." Slowly getting back to a standing position, Ev went ahead and lodged his gun back into its holster. "First, let me apologize for my partner." He turned his head to glare at her. "She acted *completely* unprofessionally."

"Got *you* to the front door." Zo gave him a proud smirk. "I'd call that a half-win."

Ev locked eyes with her. "Do you see how things are going so far?"

"Quit your squabbling, both of ya's." Earnie had raised his voice to get back on track. "Sounds like you're more than dating." Taking Evander's holstering of the gun as a peaceful cue, Earnie engaged the safety on his rifle. "Now, is anyone gonna tell me who you are and what you want before I change my mind?"

Before Zo could say a word, Ev grunted as he stuck a yielding hand in her face. "My name is Evander Evers, this is my...*associate*...Zoey Beaumont. The organization we work for will remain nameless, but it's come to their attention that time rift energy has been active in and around your property."

Chewing on his bottom lip, Earnie couldn't keep his eyes from darting around. "I've seen some of that hullabaloo on the news before. Must be some tricky stuff to deal with. But there's been nothing like that around these parts."

Zo crossed her arms as she leaned back against the deck's railing. "Oh, so those austroraptors we saw on our way in, you wouldn't happen to know anything about them, right?"

Earnie sucked in his lips to keep them from trembling. "I don't…. Uh, what did you call—"

"Not to mention a glyptodon munching on hay over by your barn. Yup, I saw it on my way in," she added, moving her head to try and maintain eye contact with the older man. "Want to reiterate your *stupid* comment from earlier?"

Holding up a defensive hand, Earnie waved it around. "Listen, I've owned this property for over fifty years now. Heck, it's been in my family for three generations." Though his legs grew tired, he did his best to stay upright and vigilant. "My ol' man, rest his soul, taught me that any creature who finds itself within this property is to be cared for and kept safe."

Zo snorted. "And yet you have 'No Trespassing' signs."

"Humans ain't animals, missy," he countered with a sly grin. "And thanks for proving that you can read."

"With all due respect, Earnest…" Ev butted in, trying to maintain some kind of amity. "…that's all fine and good. It's admirable, really." He switched gears into business mode. "The people we work for, however, have an objective to return all time-displaced creatures back to their correct time period. We believe it's what's best for the past and our present."

As the words registered in Earnie's mind, he stepped backward. "You mean, they want to take my dinosaurs and critters…away from me?"

Baffled and letting out a single chuckle, Zo piped up. "*Your* dinosaurs? These aren't your dinosaurs."

"*My* property, *my* dinosaurs."

Ev took a quick deep breath. "Respectfully, these creatures

don't belong here. They don't even belong in this time—"

"And *respectfully…*" Earnie shed a tear as he rocked back and forth on his heels. He used his barrel-up rifle stationed in front of him like a cane. "…everything I own and everything in it is mine and gives me purpose." He wiped his cheek with the back of a hand. "Gives me…*something to live for.*"

"Listen, Earnie." Zo made her voice even firmer. "Whatever attachment you may have to these animals, you can't just operate your farm like it's *Jurassic Park.*"

Getting heated, Earnie cleared his throat before staring them down. "Things are going quite fine and dandy 'round here on my *Primeval Ranch,* actually. And I plan on keeping it that way."

Finally uncrossing her arms, Zo brought herself within a foot of the elderly man. "Let's go over some details then, shall we? Do you know what to do when a dinosaur gets sick? Do you even know how to tell if they're sick?"

Earnie clenched his teeth. "Well, I—"

"And different creatures thrive in different environments," she continued, getting increasingly animated and overbearing. "Is there enough clean water, and even more importantly, how do you keep them all fed and satisfied? What about all the carnivores?"

Earnie raised his eyebrows. "Those so-called carnivores don't touch a thing unless it's died of natural causes or roadkill. Fellas leave dead animals right at the gate all the time."

She laughed in his face. "Oh, so other people know about what's going on?"

"No questions asked. I just tell 'em I've got plenty of land for burying 'em."

Shaking her head, she didn't pull away as tears of her own welled up in her eyes. "Of course you do. You think you've got all the freaking angles covered, don't you?"

Ev noted a slight shake in the ground. "Uh, Zoey."

Leaning in closer to the young woman, Earnie stood his ground. "Right, you kids always get what you want, don't ya?" He flared his nostrils and used a whiney tone. "Aw, gonna go cry to *your momma* about me?"

A piercing breath burned Zo's lungs.

Earnie broke their staring contest, becoming cognizant of her open palm less than an inch from the side of his unshaven face.

Another tremor made Ev look around. "What is that?"

"*Leave…my friend…alone!*"

A giant reptilian foot overstepped the fence alongside the house, followed by another.

Ev and Zo turned their heads as a tarbosaurus took intimidating steps toward them.

Sitting atop the dinosaur, a teenage girl manned the saddle.

"Get lost," Lucero shouted down to the unwelcome pair. "Or I'll let Tess here go hog wild on you."

Tess opened her massive jaws, showcasing her rows of teeth.

*ROOOOUUUUUUUUUUUUUH!*

Keeping a hand close to his gun, Ev couldn't take his eyes off the dinosaur. "My God."

"I've already tested out the saddle," Lucero added with a proud grin. "Another test run *wouldn't hurt.*"

"S-s-stay back," Ev pleaded before thrusting a business card toward Earnie. "In case you have any questions." Then he seized his partner's arm. "Zo, we need to go."

"She's…." Zoey glanced around at the girl, the old man, and the dinosaur, over and over again. "She…. She's *riding* it."

Guiding her away from the homestead to the driveway, Evander took one last glimpse at the tarbosaurus. "And we need to ride along outta here."

# TWENTY-ONE

**"STILL HAVEN'T** seen anything, *hermano*," Blanca, one of Alvaro's associates reported from the other side of town. "Santiago has been on highway patrol, too. Said there's been nothing."

Eating a quick lunch in the cab of his pickup truck, Alvaro took a sip of alcohol from his stainless-steel flask. He had his cellphone set to speaker mode. "There should at least be one person who saw the spino." Setting the flask back in the mid-console holder, he ran his fingers over his goatee, then gripped the steering wheel. "Why are there no signs whatsoever?"

"No idea," Blanca responded. "Any possibility *Humberto* had something to do with—"

"He was with me the *whole* time," he countered, recalling every detail from the night before. "When we left for the meeting, it was still in his trailer. The door was closed and locked."

"Okay, okay." She sighed through pinched lips. "Some have heard whispers of a new cartel making waves. And I've never quite trusted Raf."

"Raf is rough, but he's loyal," he growled back. "Always has been."

She snorted. "Loyal. That's a funny word."

"What do you mean?"

"I mean…." She let a long exhale out through her nose. "Loyalty is also a currency, and sometimes it doesn't balance out the way you think it should."

"Ah." Alvaro raised his eyebrows. "Still having some *daddy issues?*"

Blanca tapped her knife against her car's dash, wanting to plunge its blade into the upholstery. "You said Humberto has kids, right?"

He paused. "*Sí.*"

"How many?"

"Why you asking?"

"Do you want me to help or not?"

Another few seconds dragged by before he opened his mouth again. "Two. Son and daughter."

Blanca continued in detective mode. "Was she at the house *before* or *after* you and Humberto left?"

"Before." He picked up the flask, but hesitated when the opening hit his bottom lip. "When we returned…I only saw the son."

"Was she in the house?"

"She…." He rubbed his forehead, doing his best to remember the conversation. "No, but the boy said something about going to someone's place. Aaron, or something."

She took her turn to pause in thought. "What's his kids names?"

"Do you really—" Turning off the speaker mode, he whipped the phone to his ear. "Blanca, do you really want to involve these… *They're just kids* for God's sake."

"And if I was El Cazador, I'd want all the bases covered," she shot back with determination. "Wouldn't you?"

Again, silence was all he could give until he admitted, "*Sí.*"

She tapped her fingernails along her knife's blade. "I'll need their names and address."

"Just…." He tensed his jaw before taking another swig from his flask. "Remember that *we* were kids once."

"Getting *soft*, Balderos?"

"We deal with dinosaurs, *not* kids."

"I'll take that as a yes."

Cracking his neck, Alvaro closed his eyes. "Zavier and Lucero."

# TWENTY-TWO

**"ARE YOU** okay after all of that?" Back inside Earnie's house, Lucero had joined him at the island for lunch. She'd only taken tiny bites of her sandwich. "They looked like government people, or something."

Earnie sat beside her, lost in a turbulent sea of cluttered thoughts in his mind.

Leaning forward, she tried to reach his peripheral. "Earnie?"

"Hmm?"

"You've barely said a word," she reminded, trying to be as comforting as possible. "And you haven't even touched your sandwich."

"I'm…." He pushed the plate further away. "Those people coming here, talking about sending the dinos back to where they came from…. It's exactly what I'd been talking about earlier."

Confused, she turned in her chair to face him. "Earlier? What do you…." It kicked in. "Oh, that."

He rubbed the back of his neck. "Like I said before, all of this...." He flicked his hand out with half-hearted emphasis. "What we have going on here, the dinosaurs, you coming over almost every weekend..." With a sniffle, he looked at her with bittersweet, watering eyes. "...it can't last forever, as much as we want it to."

"*Please,*" she whimpered. "Don't talk like that."

"Luz." Earnie coughed out a nervous lump from his throat. "Why do you always want to come here?"

She used her finger to pick up a crumb from her plate, and placed it on her tongue. She'd blocked out certain thoughts to the point her brain knew when to shut down.

Hoping to get something out of her, he spoke softer. "Lucero?"

"It's supposed to be *fun* here," she blurted out, getting off the island stool and heading for the back door.

He swiveled to watch her march away. "Luz, come on now."

"No, *you* come on!"

Baffled by her defensive attitude, he scrunched his eyebrows together. "Lucero, I have and always will treat you like my own kin. But if you don't know by now that I want the *outright best* for you like a granddaughter, then I.... Well, I've downright *failed.*"

Her hand gripped the doorknob.

She took a tiny glance at her heartbroken reflection.

Luz let her shoulders slump forward, as well as her head. "You could *never* fail at that."

Earnie's next words came out breathy and shaky. "Then why are you treating me like I'm a dang stranger?"

Clenching her eyelids shut, she pushed tears out and onto the floor before relocating her gaze to him. Among every thought and emotion pummeling her insides like an enraged warrior, she could only open her mouth to say one thing. "I miss *her*."

Picking up on the inflection, he released his tight chest with a fast breath. "Oh, girly." Getting up, he hobbled over as fast as his aching old legs could take him. "Luz, I can only imagine."

"And I don't…have to imagine," she responded between sobs. Her body couldn't make up its mind whether to lock into place or crumble to the floor. "She's *gone* and…I can't stop being so angry about it."

About to say something, he stopped, deciding to simply be a listening ear.

"She'd always be the one I turned to, the only one I could count on." She took quick breaths as her body radiated uncomfortable heat. "There were others, but it always felt like it was her and I. Now I'm here—*by myself*—trying to keep it all together, and no one else wants to talk about it, like they don't even care." Rubbing her palms against her face, she unleashed a loud sniffle. "Everyone else shoves it all down, so I might as well do that, too, right?"

Still, he opted to be a silent friend.

"I miss her so damn much, and I feel like I failed her in so many ways. I should've fought harder to spend more time with her before…. Before she…."

Reaching out to comfort her, Earnie pulled away when she braced herself against the door.

"And being here," she continued, gazing out at the assorted primeval creatures throughout the ranch. "Being with you and these animals, with Tess…. It's a place where I can take things one day at a time, one goodbye at a time. It's a place I love to be."

He ran a hand over the top of her head before taking her free hand in both of his. "Sounds awfully familiar. We must be related."

Pushing herself off from the back door, she met his teary eyes and acknowledged who he'd referred to. "Marilyn?"

"*Marilyn.*" Saying her name made a momentary grin light up his face. "When I'd finished caring for her and giving her my all, these dinos became my new purpose." He did the same as Luz, taking in the prehistoric friends he'd made. "That day Tess and her brother hopped through that rift, I didn't know what I was gonna do." He formed another smile, easier than before. "But I could hear Marilyn's voice as if she'd been standing right beside me saying, 'Every creature is a *gift*, and it's our *responsibility* to care for them.'"

"My mom…." A warming sensation came over Luz, as if her mother's embrace had materialized to lessen the pain. "She'd probably say the same thing."

Earnie made a single chuckle. "Perhaps we really are related, then."

She spun and locked her arms around him. "You'll always be my *abuelo.*"

Surprised by her sudden movement, he laughed and returned the hug. "Aw, ain't you sweeter than a pecan pie." After rubbing her back, he cleared his throat once more.

"What's say we finish our luncheon, then we'll go check on those spikey babies again?"

Luz sniffled. "Or, we could eat our sandwiches *while* spending time with the babies."

"That's a swell idea, missy."

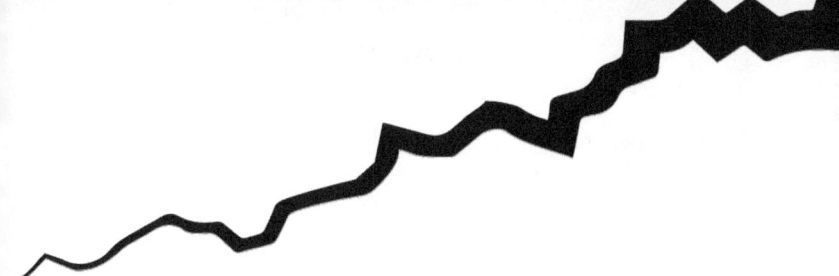

# TWENTY-THREE

**ON THEIR** way back to the hotel, neither Evander nor Zoey had said a single word to each other.

Disappointed in her earlier tactics, Evander ran scenarios in his head of how to try and patch things up with Mr. Pardy.

As for Zoey, she stewed in the passenger seat while watching the rugged Texan landscape fly by her window.

"We gonna talk about what happened back there?" Evander spoke up, somewhat casual in his delivery.

"Nope."

Ev stayed silent for a couple seconds. "Maybe we *should* ta—"

"Or maybe we could drive in *silence,*" Zo blurted out, staring out her window. "Silence can be a magnificent thing."

He grunted. "And ignorance is a blissful thing, too, right?"

Wanting to throw words back at him, she couldn't form any. She blinked rapidly as her throat tightened. Not even the scenery outside the car gave her a sense of happiness. *I should just open the door and tuck and roll out of—*

"Two years ago, my team had been sent on an op to retrieve one of our own behind enemy lines," Ev began, then checked all of his mirrors before merging into the right lane. "It was my second time in combat."

Simply listening, she now stared straight ahead.

"When we showed up…" A level of distress seeped into his voice. "…I had never seen so much blood before."

Zoey didn't realize she'd slightly angled her body toward him.

"There were five of us." Holding onto the wheel with his right hand, he rested his left elbow on the window's indoor ledge. His left hand rubbed the side of his face. "I'd been tasked with return fire. Three of my unit…they didn't make it *ten feet* from the vehicle."

She closed her eyes, becoming overwhelmed with the mounting emotion within the car. "Ev, you don't have to—"

"Me and Kenner, we were the only ones left." While retelling the events, he undid another button on his black shirt to release some heat from his chest. "I tried firing back, but I couldn't even locate where they were attacking from. Kenner tried to make for the driver's seat, the friggin' idiot…."

"Ev, stop talking."

"They peppered the windshield."

Placing her hands against the passenger dash, she released intense breaths. "*Evander.*"

"Kenner had literally just enlisted."

"*Pull...over!*"

He swerved, bringing the car onto the shoulder, and unlocked the doors.

Zoey exploded out and stumbled onto the ground. As her legs gave out, she forced her arms to keep the rest of her from hitting the dusty gravel.

Evander left the driver side, and came around to find her sobbing and hyperventilating. He lowered himself, placing a reassuring hand on her shoulder. "Breathe, Zoey. Come on, just breathe—"

"How...dare you!" She pulled away, causing her backside to fall to the ground. "Could you not tell that I didn't want to talk?"

He scowled at her. "Earlier, you said we should get to know each other."

"About literally *anything else!*" she whipped back while staggering back to a standing position. "Like, are you a morning or night person? Are you currently in a relationship? Which superpower would you choose? Pineapple on pizza, yes or no?"

"Depends on the day, teleportation, and only if there's no tomato sauce," he answered without any delays.

She tilted her head to the side. "You...didn't answer the relationship ques—"

"And before we go any further, you need to learn to keep your emotions *in check* when we're on a *goddamn mission!*"

Bringing both hands to her cheeks, she stomped two steps away before turning around. "Yeah, well *Clint Eastwood* back there, he brought up my...."

Standing between her and the car, Evander shoved his hands in his pockets.

"My…."

He gave her a gentle push. "Your mom."

Once she'd wiped some tears from her eyes, she glared at him. "How did you know about—"

"Told Seb I don't work with people unless I get their file," he answered in a nonchalant manner before switching to empathetic. "It's a horrible thing that happened to her."

"Oh, so Seb gave you *my* file, but he gave me *zilch* on you?"

"You could've asked."

Raking fingers through her hair, she squeezed her eyelids closed. "Do I even need to tell you anything about me then? How much of what happened was in the file?"

He raised an eyebrow. "Dawn Beaumont, worked for pre-incident SauraCorps as a veterinarian. Post-incident SauraCorps, she also became an operative for high-risk assignments. Killed in action by ex-SauraCorps member Blake Arrowsmith."

A whimper was all she could respond with.

He lowered his head and looked at the pebbles around his feet. "And now you work for SauraCorps to live up to her name."

"To stop more Arrowsmiths and disgusting humans like him from exploiting and hurting these animals," she added, finally able to form a cohesive sentence. "And to stop them from *hurting families*…like he did mine."

Ev nodded. "There's nothing wrong with honoring those we've lost. But when we're out in the field, *you*…."

He cracked his neck, trying to release some tension. "*We* cannot let those emotions compromise the mission."

Zoey pursed her lips. "Guess I did get him a little riled up."

He squinted one eye at her. "You trespassed onto his property, then almost assaulted him when he pushed the wrong button."

"I would've slapped him."

"*Assault.*"

"To-may-to, to-mah-to."

Evander took a deep breath. "If anything like that happens again, I'm requesting to work with someone else."

# TWENTY-FOUR

"**YESENIA,** *linda,* we still good for tonight?" Zavier played with the front of his hair while checking himself over in a full-length mirror.

"Are we doing a fancy place or casual?" Yesenia inquired, trying to ready herself. "Need to figure out an outfit."

"Girl, you look fancy in anything and everything." He added a single suave chuckle at the end of his smooth delivery.

"That's sweet, but doesn't help."

"Also, my dad is out and won't be back until late tonight." He added more charm as he spoke. "And Luz is at Earnie's, so I was *thinking....*"

She snickered. "That you should get me home at a *respectable* hour, or else my dad will feed you to our Mastiff?"

"Churro loves me. He'll just lick me to dea—"

*Knock-knock-knock.*

Zav heard the noise, but couldn't see the front of the

house from his window. "I think someone's at the front door, but go for fancy. See you in an hour, *hermosa.*"

"Bye, Zavvy-wavvy."

Already heading down the stairs, he grinned. "Love you more than Hollywood loves rebooting stuff we don't want!" Hanging up and in a lovey daze, he didn't check the side windows before opening the door.

"*Where is she?*"

He froze. "Daira? What are you—"

"Luz isn't answering my texts *at all,*" Daira blurted out, storming past him into the house. "And I am *not leaving* until her and I talk."

"She isn't here, and probably won't be back until tomorrow night." He lifted his open palms into the air while following Daira up the stairs. "Also, I know about *Ollie.* Can't believe you did that to—"

"And that's why we *need* to talk," she pleaded, getting frazzled. "Everything is so wrong right now, and *stupid*-complicated…" Turning around at Luz's bedroom door, she gazed up into his enraged hazel eyes. "…and I can't just stand by and watch our friendship fall apart."

Zav simmered down a bit as he picked up on the hurt in her voice. "Look, I wish I could help out, but I've got a date in—"

*Knock-knock-knock!*

They both looked toward the front door.

"Who is it now?" Reluctant, Zav made it to the top of the stairs and paused. *What if the cartel figured things out and returned?* He turned around and waved Daira back. "Go into Luz's room."

"Why would I—"

"Just *trust me* and go."

Marching down the stairs, he made a mental note to identify the visitor first. He peeked through the side window as he approached the door.

A woman with long, dark hair and wearing a faded leather jacket stood outside. She leaned to the side, peering through the door's side window.

Getting an odd vibe, Zav opened the door a smidge. "Hello?"

The woman straightened her stance. "Is this the Sanchez residence?"

"Depends, are you selling something, wanting to talk about Jesus, or both?"

"I'm Blanca," she revealed in a solemn tone. "I work with your father, and—" She glanced around the inside of the house from her vantage point. "Is your sister home, too?"

"Uh…" With the possibility of Humberto working for a cartel, Zav opted to play along in his own way. He also pretended Daira wasn't currently upstairs. "It's just me at the moment. She went out, but I have no idea where."

Still within earshot, Daira picked up on his lie in order to keep her safe.

"Oh." Blanca placed one of her hands in her jacket pocket. "Well…I hate to be the one to tell you this, but *something happened* to your dad on his way in to work."

"What?" He gave her a puzzled and slightly suspicious look as he opened the door further. "He *literally* left almost half an hour ago—"

"And there was an accident," Blanca added, struggling to keep impatience at bay. "He's on his way to the hosp—"

"If you don't mind…" Zav pulled out his cellphone with confidence. "…I'm gonna call him right—"

*BzZzZzZzZzT!*

"—now-*ow-ow!*"

Blanca tasered him in the neck before he could bring the phone to his ear.

He collapsed to the tile floor.

Upstairs, Daira clasped a hand to her mouth. Deep inside, her sisterly friendship with him compelled her to help, while her preservation side kept her feet planted.

Blanca lifted Zavier up with his arm over her shoulders. "All right, smart guy, you're coming with me."

# TWENTY-FIVE

**HAULING SOME** roadkill and animal carcasses in the bucket of a compact front loader, Earnie drove it slow and careful. He brought it around to the side of the barn opposite from his house. Once he'd made it to the usual feeding spot, he dumped the pile of remains, reversed back about twenty feet, and shut off the engine.

"Gotta love the smell of rotting flesh in the afternoon," Lucero remarked, pulling her shirt up and over her nose.

"These dinos definitely do." Earnie hopped out of the machine nice and easy. "Nature's cleanup crew."

Already nearby, Tess and her brother thundered over. It hadn't taken long for them to be lured by the stench of death.

"Tango sure looks hungry." Luz backed up a tad, giving the dinosaurs more room. She noticed the resident pack of three austroraptors swiftly darting around rocks and brush as they approached the mound of flesh and bones. "Aramis, Porthos, and Athos are right on time."

Earnie wiped his brow and fanned his arms around to cool down. "They'll be picking out the 'coons, rabbits, and smaller giblets again, I'm sure."

She snorted. "Don't say giblets."

"Why not? You know it means innards and—"

"I know what it means." She stuck her tongue out in disgust. "It's up there with gross words like viscera and... *moist.*"

He chuckled. "Kids these days, always making up new...."

Leaves on the few surrounding trees had started to flutter.

Even with old legs, Earnie could pick up a slight tremor in the ground. "What in the world?"

"I feel it, too." Luz grabbed onto him to try and keep both of them steady. "What the heck is it? An earthquake?"

Getting spooked, most of the creatures in the vicinity began fleeing.

With their backs up against the barn wall, Earnie and Luz detected a concentrated airflow tugging at their clothing.

*CRRRRACK-ACK-ACK! ZAP! CRACKLE! SNAP!*

"Another rift!" Luz yelled out in sheer awe. "Haven't seen one in...a year?"

Gazing at the gigantic circular electrical opening, Earnie placed a hand to his chest. "Magnificent."

*BWOOM! BWOOM! BWOOM!*

Moving closer to the rift, Luz peeked through the space-time window. "Holy...a big one's making an entrance!"

A dinosaur's head poked through, followed by a long, slender neck. Its bulky body carried on with reverberating steps, and its lengthy tail carried a club with minor spikes.

"My, my, my." Earnie had an open-mouthed grin. "Never seen one of those before."

"Wait, I'll try to look it up." Luz opened a search engine on her phone. "Long-necked dinosaur with club tail."

Pictures and articles popped up.

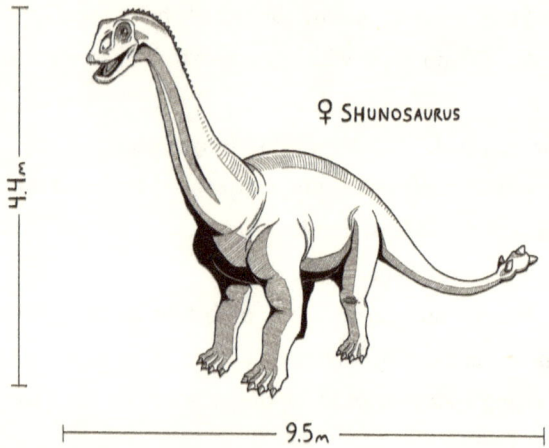

♀ SHUNOSAURUS

4.4m

9.5m

"That looks like the one." She showed the screen to her older friend. "Shunosaurus—wait, *shu-noh-sore-us*—from the mid-Jurassic, and originally from the Sichuan province of China."

"Shoot." He smirked. "We ain't got a Chinese restaurant for many miles."

She slapped him while laughing. "Your jokes are getting worse with age."

*Z-Z-ZAP! ZZZZEEEEUUUU-POP!*

The rift shrank inward into thin air.

Startled by the closing rift, the shunosaurus wailed and stomped its front feet.

Alarmed, Luz withdrew a step. "Shoot, it's spooked—

*whoa, watch out!"*

The forty-foot-long Shunosaurus whipped its tail toward the humans, who ducked and split just in time. Agitated, it swung its head around, uncomfortable with the new surroundings and unfamiliar beings.

Earnie barely made it to the barn's large open door. "Luz, get in here!"

Scrambling to get back up, she made sure to watch out for the spiked club tail. "We need to find a way to calm it down." Sprinting to get in front of the scared dinosaur, she held her open palms up. "Hey, down here!"

"*Luz!*" Earnie hollered again, waving an insistent hand. "What in God's name are you doing?"

She shouted back, "I'm hoping—"

*BWOOM!*

As the shunosaurus slammed a foot into the ground, Luz stumbled backward.

Her eyes opened wide.

The dinosaur's left front foot loomed overtop of her.

*BWOOOOM!*

Luz had rolled out of the way with an inch to spare.

Earnie winced, blocking his view with an arm. Opening his eyes, he released a thankful sigh for seeing his young friend still alive. "You're gonna get yourself killed."

"It needs to know we're friendly."

*WHA-BAM!*

Wood splintered as the shunosaurus's clubbed tail hammered the barn door right above Earnie's head.

Retreating further into the barn, Earnie took labored

breaths. Dizziness overcame him, along with a slight numbness in his face. As he slumped onto the dirt floor to rest, he did his best to keep an eye on the spike lodged deep into the sliding door.

Unable to pull its tail away, the shunosaurus became even more agitated.

Back on her feet, Luz removed her flannel overshirt while sprinting for the door. *Hope this works.* She dodged one of the back feet, made it to the tail, then jumped up to catch the other spike. Clambering up onto the club, she gripped the tail and shimmied forward.

Detecting the girl's weight, the dinosaur wobbled back and forth, trying to shake her off.

Luz launched herself onto its main body and managed to find her footing. Every lunge forward brought her closer to the neck. *Almost there.*

*AAAAWNK-AAAAWNK!*

Rearing up, the shunosaurus used its weight to thrust its front legs to the ground.

The shuddering movement launched Luz forward.

Using the overshirt still in her hand, she swung it over the base of the neck. She barely snagged one of the arms of her shirt with her left hand, making her back hit the dinosaur's chest. Dangling there, she laughed to herself. "Can't believe…that actually wor—*ooooooa!*"

Again, the shunosaurus lifted its front end up and slammed its feet back down. Lowering its head in the process, it forced Luz to slide.

Making it to the base of its head, she engaged her abs to

shimmy the jacket up and over the creature's eyes. "Okay, time to calm down." Tying the arms together, she used the last of her energy to haul herself up and onto its crest. Gently patting and rubbing the dinosaur's face, she lowered her voice to a soothing tone. "We're not going to hurt you."

*Aaaaaaaawnk.*

Slowly, the shunosaurus dropped its head closer to the mix of grass and dirt.

"That's it," Luz whispered, reaching down to pat the tip of its snout. "There's nothing to be afraid of here."

"Lu...*Luz....*"

She snapped her head up, picking up on the echo of his voice. "Earnie? Are you still in the barn?"

"L-Luz...." He strained himself to speak up. "I n-n-need...you...here."

Immediately sliding off the dinosaur's head, she dashed over and into the barn. She found him laying on his side. "*¡Ay, Dios mío! Earnie!*" Coming to his aid, she helped him to sit up. "What happened to you?"

"S-s-s-stroke." Blinking rapidly, he managed to turn his head. "There's t-t-two of y-you."

As much as part of Luz wanted to freeze in panic, her mind raced through all the things that could or should be done. "We gotta get you to the hospital. Can you stand—"

"No...ho-hospital."

"But if you've just had a stroke—"

"N-n-*no.*"

"Earnie, this could lead to complica—"

"Luc-c-cero, I'll be f-fine," he retorted, waving his good

hand in a dismissive manner. "It's just...a s-small one." Using his good hand to pinch the bridge of his nose, he forced a longer breath out of his lungs. "Happened before."

Her anxious eyebrows ached from tension. "Before? When I'm not around?"

"Don't wo-worry about me." Breathing normally now, he gazed over at the open doorway. "How's the d-dino?"

After examining him up and down, she took his impaired hand in hers. "I managed to cover its eyes. Since it's worked on others, figured I'd give it a try on this one."

"Well...I'll be." Earnie snickered. "Luz the dino wrangler." He finally met her concerned hazel eyes. "This ranch definitely needs...*needs* you."

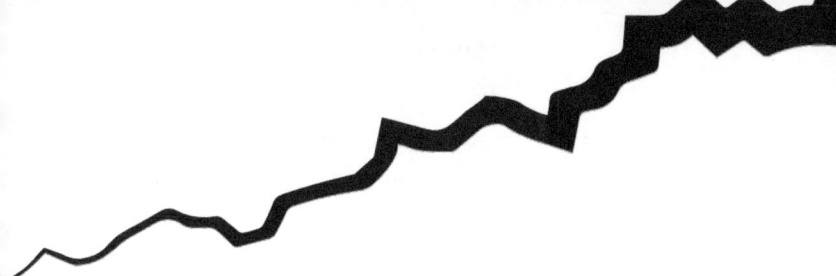

# TWENTY-SIX

**HEADING NORTH** for the city of Alpine, Evander and Zoey watched for a local restaurant they'd discovered online as they gave their SauraCorps superior a detailed report of events.

Hooked up by Bluetooth, Sebastian's voice spoke through the car's speakers. "Zoey, you almost assaulted an eighty-year-old man?"

"To be fair, he nearly shot one of us," she countered while taking in the scenic route. "I would've called it self-defense."

"Right. And this girl was...*riding* the dinosaur?"

"With a saddle and everything," Ev added, making an impressed grunt. "Like a cowgirl in the Wild West. Looked like some kind of t-rex—"

"Tarbosaurus," Zo informed, completely casual about it. "Probably still in its juvenile years, or close to adult."

Ev recalled the size of it. "How was that a juvey? It was huge."

Getting to flex her intellect, she spoke matter-of-factly. "Larger dinosaurs, even long-necked sauropods, can grow at fourteen kilograms a day. Training a dinosaur to accept a saddle and even learn to be jockeyed, it's better to start them young."

"Refocus here, guys." Sebastian sighed through his nose. "Now to figure out a way to deal with this more amicably."

Ev pulled into a parking lot for the restaurant. "Already planning on heading back tomorrow morning…*alone.*"

"Oh really?" Zo twisted in her seat. "Think you can get through to the man from *UP* on your own, huh?"

Ev rested both hands on the steering wheel. "I'll get through with words, not hands like *someone* tried to—"

"Man, I never thought pairing you two up would go like this," Sebastian piped up, getting ready to end the call. "Let me know how it goes, Ev. Hopefully we can send in more people sooner than later."

Zo unclipped her seatbelt. "See you, Se—"

*Click.*

The call ended.

"Awesome." She released her jaw muscles, finally realizing how much they had been hurting. *Now both of them don't believe in me.*

Evander stepped out of Betty and stretched as he stood. An enticing aroma of chilis, spices, cooked corn, and assorted meats all wafted around his nose. "Smells fantastic."

Following suit, Zo slammed her door shut more forceful than usual. "Smells like you're looking for a new partner."

He placed a foot on the front patio's step, then turned to

find her much closer than he'd expected. "Look, if you—"

She put up a hand to maintain some distance, which had ended up pressing against his taut chest by accident. "Sorry, I didn't—oh, my God. How much do you bench?"

He stared at her hand.

She pulled it away, getting flustered. "Sorry."

"It's...fine, just...." He noticed behind the fluster an underlying frustration in her intense turquoise eyes. "If... you can control that temper of yours, then you're more than welcome to come along."

She looked up into his concerned chocolate eyes. Something about his tone gave her a sense of protection and the possibility of actual camaraderie. "I will...do my best."

Ev grinned. "Which will hopefully be better than today."

With a cheeky smirk on her face, Zo followed him into the restaurant. "Also, seriously, how much do you bench? Because I've felt a decent number of pecs in my day and yours are impressive."

Opening the main door, he whipped a surprised glance at her. "Did that question *actually* come out of your mouth?"

More Mexican cuisine aromas hit her nose, making her salivate instantly. "What? Personally, I can get a good eighty pounds on a good day."

Sliding into a booth, he studied her physique a little more as she took the seat across from him. "Never took you for the gym kind." He accepted a menu from the waitress. "With your energy and wild streak, would've thought you'd be in something like roller derby."

"No thank you," she laughed in reply. "I'm not a *Whip*

*It* girl."

Perusing the list of food, he glanced up at her with a grin. "Is that some kind of movie reference?"

"That *is* the movie." Also checking their lunch options, she arched an eyebrow. "Maybe when we get back to the hotel room, I'll get you properly cultured."

He grunt-laughed. "I'm more cultured than you think."

"Really?" She lowered the laminated piece of paper. "Finish this sentence: My name is Inigo Montoya—"

"You killed my father." Evander continued the *Princess Bride* line without missing a beat, and leaned forward. "Prepare to die."

Zoey threw both hands up in a victorious gesture. "*Inconceivable!*"

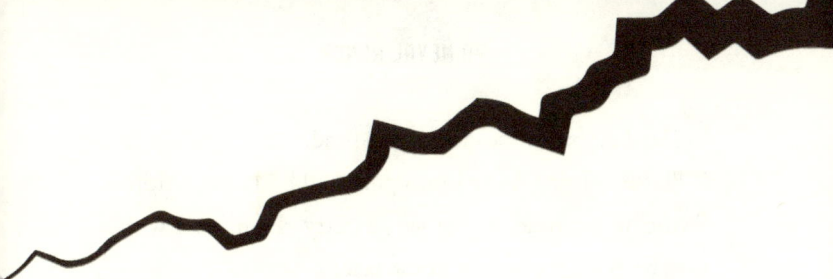

# TWENTY-SEVEN

**DARKNESS.**

Turning his head left and right, Zavier couldn't see a thing. *Did I just get...kidnapped?* He replayed the freshest memories in his mind. *Dad left, Daira came over looking for Luz, and...some chick named Blanca?* The last unfortunate event came back to him. *She tased me.* He noticed a wetness in his lap. *Must've peed my freaking pants agai—*

*BRRAAAAUUUUGH!*

He immediately flinched in the chair he'd been tied to. *"Jeeeesucristo!"*

A low grumble and snort came from somewhere close to him.

"H-hey." Shaking, he hoped another human would be in the room. "Is someone out there?"

No one answered.

"If you're planning on scaring me more, I'll warn you, my bladder isn't quite empty—"

The dark bag whooshed off his head.

Harsh lighting made him squint and blink on overdrive. Swinging his head to the left, a furry rhino head with a massive horn stared him in the face.

♂ ELASMOTHERIUM
"WOOLLY RHINO"

2.0m

4.5m

*BRRAAAAUUUUGH!*

"*Aaaaaah!* Put it back on!" he screamed out, trying to fight against his restraints. "Put the headcover back on!"

"Relax." Blanca had raised her voice to grab his attention. "It's in a cage."

Taking a moment to take in his whereabouts, he noticed the metal bars between him and the woolly rhino. "So it is." He'd been taken to a warehouse of some sort. More cages made up most of the decor, housing some creatures he'd recognized, and others he didn't. "Is it just me, or did you mistake me for a dinosaur? I don't think I really belong—"

"Tell me everything you know," Blanca demanded, leaning against an unused cage.

He gulped, attempting to keep himself composed. "Everything?"

Her upper lip twitched. "Everything."

Glancing to the right, he noticed a confined theropod with white scales and blueish-grey lines running down the length of its body. In another large cage, a pair of oversized wolves paced back and forth.

He gave his head a slight shake. *We were right. It is a cartel.*

Blanca pulled out her combat knife, letting the blade flash off the inside lights. "Need a little *encouragement?*"

"Okay…. Okay."

At that moment, his mind replaced Blanca with his mother. He imagined Hana reaching out and raising his chin with a loving hand. It took him back to his last moments with her, when she'd said: *Keep being brave, Zavier. Be brave for me, and be brave for them. And don't ever lose that childish charm I love so much.*

A wave of boldness came over him. He shook less, his voice lost its tremor. Nodding, he kept one thing on his mind. *Family is everything, and I'll die for them.*

Blanca stepped forward. "So?"

"You really mean…everything?"

Glaring at him, she flared her nostrils. "Quit delaying, or I'll start with cutting off—"

"Rubber bands last longer when refrigerated," he blurted out, keeping as straight a face as possible. "If you plug your nose, you can't tell the difference between an apple, an onion, and a potato."

Blanca's glare morphed into bewilderment. "Excuse me?"

"Did you know it's possible to turn peanut butter into diamonds?"

"What are you—"

"You spend ninety-two days of your life on the toilet."

She stomped forward. "Stop spewing nonsense and tell me—"

"And sloths can hold their breath longer than dolphins, which is really quite amaz—"

*Thwack!*

Blanca backhanded him in the face. "Give me something *useful,* you little twirp."

"Ow, God…." He worked the sting from his face. "Twirp… is the noise you make…when you fart in a bathtub full of water—"

*Smack!*

"*Aaaa-ha-ha-ooow!*" Dazed by the throbbing, he let his head slump forward. "Really? The diamond thing would be useful for a cartel—oh, *crap.*"

"And there it is." Finally grinning, she spun the knife around her hand and caught it with ease. "Now, what really happened with the spinosaurus last night?"

Zavier rolled his head to the left and looked the woolly rhino in the eye once more. Trapped like the rest of the helpless prehistoric animals, he didn't see any way out of his bindings or the warehouse. "Might as well kill me, then."

Outside the warehouse and down the street by half a block, Daira sat in her car. Thankfully, she hadn't been noticed tailing the strange woman. She'd watched the lady drag an unconscious Zavier inside the unassuming building.

Her instincts told her to call Lucero.

But her best friend's silence told Daira it would be of no use.

*Ten more minutes,* she told herself. *And if there's no sign of Zav, or if Luz doesn't answer….*

A sense of urgency and fear waged war inside of her.

*Good thing my baseball gear is in the trunk.*

# TWENTY-EIGHT

**"DO YOU** think more rifts might open up around here?" Lucero sipped on some afternoon sweet tea up on the back deck. She could see the shunosaurus's head off in the distance. "Maybe more dinosaurs are popping up around here than we thought."

Taking a gulp from his own glass, Earnie sat back in his lounge chair. "Last one close to this spot was right inside the barn, when Tess and Tango landed here."

Luz rubbed the side of her drink with her thumb. "The news hasn't reported any rifts in a long time."

He closed his eyes and tipped his safari-style hat over his face. "Perhaps they ain't looking in the right spots."

Standing against the railing, she turned back. "Those two people from earlier found us." She swished the tea around. "If they knew dinosaurs were here, what's stopping others from finding that out, too?"

He sighed from under the hat. "Let's just hope it doesn't

come to—"

*Buzzzz. Buzzzz.*

Luz's cellphone came to life while laying on the wooden railing. Lifting it to check the caller ID, she lightly bit down on her bottom lip.

### Daira Ramirez

She tapped the phone a couple times before swiping the green button. "Daira, hey, I—"

"Zav's in *trouble*," Daira announced right away, her voice drowning in dread. "Some lady came to your house and tased him, and now he's—"

"Hold on, he's *what?*" Almost knocking her glass over, Luz brought a hand to the side of her head. "He...." She put a couple of pieces together. "Wait, you came to my house?"

"Listen, I'm not gonna waste time." Daira collected herself, then proceeded to explain. "Ollie showed up at my place telling me you two weren't together anymore."

Luz slapped the railing. "Are you freaking kidding—"

"He said he'd only been seeing you to hopefully win me over one day."

Closing her eyes, Luz combed her fingers back into her hair. "I...can't believe him."

"Now, Luz, you know I have never and would never flirt with him because we're *basically hermanas*." Daira hoped her tenderness and adoration could be clearly heard. "And when he tried to lean in and kiss me, I—"

"He *what?*"

"I pulled away immediately and slapped him upside the head."

Finding it difficult to form words, Luz could only cry into the phone.

"He spread lies about it at school," Daira continued, filling in the blanks. "Kept telling everyone how I'd been 'so happy to finally have him all to myself.' I tried, but I couldn't stop it from blowing up."

Attentive to Luz's crying, Earnie lifted his hat. "Luz? What's got you all teary-eyed? What's wrong?"

Luz simply stood there. Her brain had already begun shutting down and shutting out the overwhelming emotions she didn't want to feel. Betrayal, fury, misery, and denial, among countless other things. Even the lingering loss of her mom crept back up, threatening to shove her into an abyss of despair.

"Luz?" Daira attempted to get her attention again. "Are we…still good?"

"I…." Luz croaked out, then sucked in a sharp breath. "I thought I'd *lost* you, too."

"No, no no no no." With a softened tone, Daira responded with conviction. "You are my sister, and you could *never* lose me."

Luz choked out a sob, unable to keep herself composed.

"But we have to figure out how to save Zavier, so we don't lose him." Sniffling along with her friend, Daira paused before continuing. "He's my family just as much as you are."

Coming up beside his young friend, Earnie placed a hand on Luz's shoulder. "Who is that?" He gave her shoulder a comforting squeeze. "Is there anything I can do to help?"

Turning to him, she pulled her phone away to wipe her face with the back of her arm. "Zav's in trouble, someone from the cartel must've kidnapped him."

"Shoot." Earnie braced against the railing. "Is he hurt?"

Luz enabled the speakerphone option. "Daira, Earnie's here, too. Anything else you can tell us about Zav? Is he okay?"

"He's in some kind of sketchy warehouse," Daira reported, doing her best to stay incognito in her car. "Last I saw was some lady dragging him inside over half an hour ago."

Shaking his head, Earnie fished a hand into a pocket of his overalls. "Are you safe, uh, Daira, is it? Are you close?"

"Been staking things out in my car about a block away."

"Whatever you do, missy, *do not* leave your car," Earnie ordered, hoping both teenagers would come out of the situation safe and sound. "And if anyone sees you, scream outta there like a freaking banshee and don't look back."

Luz piped up. "Send us the address so we can come—"

"Oh, *we* won't be going," he countered, pulling out a business card. "It's not safe."

Narrowing her gaze to the card, Luz didn't recognize the info on it. "Who are you calling?"

Earnie smirked. "Something tells me even our enemies have enemies."

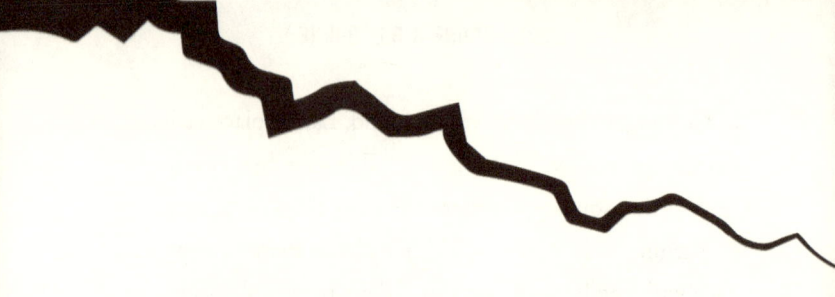

# TWENTY-NINE

**A LITTLE** over a block away and on the opposite side of the street from their current mission, Evander and Zoey scoped things out from his Mercedes.

Holding binoculars up, Ev spied the entrance to the restaurant Alvaro visited often. "No sign of Balderas yet."

"He could already be inside." Zo scanned the surrounding area, only to find nothing out of the ordinary. "I could go for a cocktail."

He snorted. "We just had lunch about—"

*GRRRROOOOUUUUWR!*

A suped-up truck hauling an oversized trailer drove past them.

Something inside the trailer had made the monstrous noise.

The truck pulled around a corner and out of view.

Ev reached for his keys still in the ignition. "Sounded like a dinosaur."

"Those are the plates we have on record," Zo added,

checking the intel. "Alvaro must be grabbing something quick. Let's get in there and—"

"Wait!" Ev grabbed her arm, keeping her from leaving the vehicle. "Zo, we can't just go charging in there. The whole place could be crawling with his crew."

She winked at him. "Don't worry, *babe,* I've got a plan."

Her word choice made his brain short-circuit. "You—what? Did you just… Why'd you call me *that?*"

Slipping her arm out of his grasp, she chuckled at his flustered response. "Follow me and you'll find out, Stud Muffin."

His cellphone vibrated from his jacket pocket as he exited the car. The caller wasn't in his contacts, but he answered anyway. "Evander. Who's this?"

"I'd say, 'the old man you terrorized earlier,' but I'm pretty sure Tess did most of the terrorizing," an older voice answered.

Zo took Ev's arm and slid her hand into his. "Who is it, Pookie?"

"Earnest?" Ev immediately changed his thought process while reacting to his partner's touch. "Zoey, just…give me—sorry, Earnest. Gotta say, I'm surprised to be hearing from you so soon."

Earnie sighed. "Well, time is of the essence, I'm afraid."

Making it across the road and less than a block away from the restaurant, Ev halted. "Is there something I can help you with?"

"My friend here who was riding the dinosaur, her brother was kidnapped earlier today," Earnie reported with complete unease. "You aware of a particular cartel in the area?"

Ev glanced at Zo and in the direction of the restaurant. "Funny you should mention that."

"We got reason to believe the kidnapper works for 'em." With more distress swelling within his tone, Earnie hoped to build some kind of trust. "Brother's name is Zavier Sanchez. I have the address, and if you can get him back to us..." He paused, mustering up boldness. "...then I'm willing to have a chat."

Ev grit his teeth together as he considered how close they were to Alvaro. "Send me the address."

"I'll get my friend to tex-mex it to you."

"Did he just say he was going to *tex-mex* me?" Evander mumbled as he ended the call and turned to Zoey. "Listen, this little plan of yours, we need to make it quick."

She resumed walking toward their current mission. "That was the *get off my ranch* guy?"

"Someone from the cartel abducted the girl's brother," he relayed, his head swirling with scenarios that could occur. Losing his team in a horrific blaze of gunfire had been one thing. Potentially losing a teenager would weigh on him even more. "We need to save that kid asap."

"Then follow my lead, *Sugar Bear.*"

Accessing the kitchen from the rear of the building, Alvaro handed a wad of cash over to the head chef. Humberto carried a small animal crate as they entered a secret room via a false walk-in freezer door.

Three men had been waiting inside.

"*Guten Tag, zusammen.*" Alvaro smiled at his German contacts. "I hope you haven't been waiting too long, Reinhardt."

The Germans' superior stood up from his chair to shake hands. "Not long. You have the feathered dinosaurs?"

Humberto lifted the crate in response. "The archaeopteryx pair are in perfect condition."

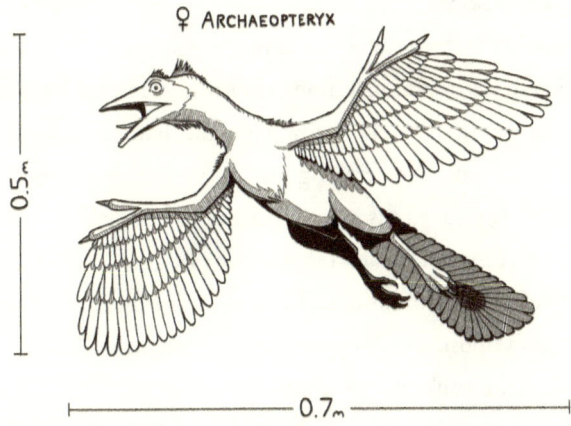

♀ ARCHAEOPTERYX

0.5 m

0.7 m

Both of the raven-sized winged dinosaurs cowered inside of their small prison. Huddled together, they flinched when the German came into view through the slats.

Reinhardt crouched and tapped his finger against the carrier's metal door. "What you call them?"

"Uh, how do I...." Humberto reiterated the name phonetically. "Aar-kee-ahp-tur-icks."

"Whatever." Reinhardt waved a hand, only interested in acquiring them for his collection. "Heinrich, give these men their money, and we will talk some more business."

"I swear, you are the *entire package,* and I'm gonna have you shipped to my place." She laughed before taking a generous sip of her jalapeño margarita while seated at the bar. "Oh, you know what we should do for our next date? There's nothing more romantic and thrilling than making out while skydiving."

The bartender gave her an amused look.

Ev did his best to play along after taking a sip of his beer. "Actually, uh...I think I know a guy for that."

She gasped. "No freaking way." Exaggerating a squeal, she lightly slapped his arm. "That would be epic!"

One of the patrons had their phone ring.

Taking a swig of his beer, Ev used his peripheral to check the man's position. "Haven't jumped out of a plane in a while. Sure you're up for that?"

Leaning in close to his face, she bit her bottom lip. "You already make my heart race, so bring on more adrenaline." From her vantage point, she observed the phone call recipient leave his table and disappear into a little hallway where restrooms were located.

Gulping down most of the remainder of her drink, Zo winked at the bartender and tugged on Ev's wrist. "How about we go somewhere a little more private?"

He gave her an alarmed glance before resorting to skittish as he slid off the stool. "Whoa, *babe*...are you...sure about this?"

She led him over to the public restroom area and made a cutesy giggle. "What can I say? I can't control myself when I'm around you." Getting to the mini hallway out of everyone else's view, she dropped the flirty act and glance-peeked through a circular window in one of the doors. "Perfect." She turned back to him. "Hope you've taken some acting classes, Sweet Cheeks."

Unable to follow any of her thought process, he blinked rapidly. "Zoey, *what on earth*—"

"*Chill,*" she whispered while putting her hair into a ponytail. "Kitchen access is right across from us."

He raised an eyebrow as he spied cooking utensils and freezer doors on the other side of the small window. "Oh, you're *good.*"

First to leave the private room, Alvaro held the door open for Humberto, who now possessed a briefcase full of money. Letting the fake freezer door close, they headed for the exit.

*BA-DUM!*

Evander and Zoey burst in, wrapped up in each other's arms.

Humberto and Alvaro spun around, ready to use their guns.

"Oh my God!" Zo pulled her face away from Ev's cheek. "Babe...." She gasped in response to him giving her neck kisses and surveyed how many people were in the room.

"We seem to…have gotten…carried away."

Concluding that the intruding couple were simply drunk and overly affectionate, Humberto smirked as he held back from revealing his weapon. "Lovebirds."

Ev glanced to the side and spotted Alvaro—their man of interest.

"We gotta *sell* this," he mumble-whispered.

Zo gazed right into his eyes. "*Bring it, Casanova.*"

Cradling her head in his hand, Ev plunged his lips into hers.

Both of them let go of their inhibitions for the moment and enjoyed the kiss. The longer they lingered in each other's embrace, the easier it was to cross the line from pretending to reality. An unidentifiable spark flashed between them.

One of the line cooks pulled out his phone and snapped a pic.

The freezer door opened again and the Germans marched out.

Heinrich glared at them. "Who is this—"

*BLAM!*

Ev swiftly unleashed his gun, shooting the German superior in the abdomen and ducking to avoid return fire.

Zo took shelter from behind the kitchen cabinets, snatching a stainless-steel pan on her way down. "Makeouts and gunfire, best date ever!"

Alvaro blasted two bullets at them and dashed for the door.

Tailing behind, Humberto tucked the briefcase under his arm.

The other two Germans exited the back room and opened fire.

Peeking over the metal cabinet, Zo used the frying pan as a shield. "We have to go—"

*BLAM-PING!*

The bullet deflected into the head chef, making him collapse.

"Jeez!" Zo hid again before readying herself to bolt. "Alvaro's getting away."

A bullet whizzed past Ev's head before he shot back, hitting the second German in the abdomen. "I'll cover you!"

Zo sprinted after the cartel members with her trusty pan in hand.

Keeping her safe from behind, Ev finished off the two German goons.

Holding onto the handle of the archaeopteryx crate, Reinholdt used it as a deterrent to protect his upper body.

Ev chuckled. "Aw, you shouldn't have."

*BLAM-BLAM-CRUNCH!*

*AAAAAAAAAUUUGH!*

Reinholdt's right knee gave way as he flopped to the hard kitchen floor. The crate crashed beside him, opening its grated door.

The two small dinosaurs poked their feathered heads out.

Hurrying over to keep the archaeopteryx pair contained, Ev half-grinned at the wounded man. "You Germans and your Wilhelm screams."

Outside, Alvaro and Humberto scrambled into the pickup truck.

"Get going, *get going!*" Humberto clutched the briefcase full of cash. "Are those the SauraCorps people?"

Pushing the engine start button, Alvaro grit his teeth. "Told you they'd be a threat." He glanced to his left side mirror.

Zoey skulked up the side of the hefty trailer.

"This *chica* needs to get *lost.*" Alvaro leaned out the open window and aimed his gun.

Diving between the truck and the trailer, Zo managed to dodge his attempts.

Grumbling expletives, Alvaro swung his rage-filled gaze over to Humberto. "Don't just sit there, help me take her out!"

Rotating in his seat, Humberto opened the passenger door.

*WHUMP-CRACK!*

Evander had bodychecked the door back into Humberto's head, putting him into a daze. "A headache worse than a bottle of tequila—"

*BLAM-BLAM!*

Having left the driver's seat, Alvaro fired from across the truck bed, making Ev duck for cover.

Hiding behind the tailgate, Zo hyped herself up by taking rapid breaths. Hustling out and toward Alvaro, she sounded a war cry. Facing his gun, she swung the pan upward for a backhand blow in tandem with him taking another shot.

The disorienting blast made her ears ring.

Her pan-work knocked the gun from Alvaro's hand.

Taking the opportunity, Alvaro disarmed her of the frying pan, snagged her hair, and tightened his grasp. He sank his free fist into her gut twice, knocking the air right out of her lungs. Latching his hand into her hair, he brought her face closer to his and snarled, "*Senorita,* you picked the *wrong* cartel to mess wi—"

"Take your frigging hands *off her,*" Ev roared, coming around the front of the truck. "Or I swear to God, I'll deliver a world of hurt."

"Back off, *gringo,*" Alvaro barked in reply. "Now, if you both were to leave us be and head on home, no one has to die today." He yanked on Zo's hair again, making her yelp while keeping her in check. "Might even be some money in it for you."

"Not how this works, Balderas," Ev warned, aiming his gun at his enemy's chest. "You'll see less prison time if you give us everything you know."

Alvaro laughed. "I'd be dead before I could tell you anything."

Ev grunted. "If you play nice, we can protect you."

"You don't get it." Alvaro pulled Zo in front of him, using her as a human shield. "My crew, this cartel, and its associates, it goes deeper than you could ever imagine." He glanced around with a craze in his eyes. "We're probably being watched right now."

Ev didn't give in to the likely distraction. "Let her go."

Alvaro's scowl morphed into an ominous smirk. "Neither of you will walk away from this alive."

*THWACK!*

He slammed Zo's head backward into the side of the truck before diving to the ground to snatch his gun. Springing back up, he took a quick shot.

Ev fired back, grazing the side of Alvaro's arm as a bullet lodged into his own bicep. "*Gaaaah*—frig sakes!"

With both Americans down or injured, Alvaro sprinted for his truck. Whipping the door open for defense, he grinned at them. "Word of advice, leave town and don't look ba—"

*BLAM!*

Alvaro gasped for air and slumped forward to the asphalt.

Zo immediately looked to her partner. "Did you…."

Staring at the dead cartel member, Ev shook his head. "Wasn't me."

They looked into the cab of the truck.

Humberto's shaky hand held a gun. With tears in his eyes and his kids on his mind, he'd pulled the trigger. "I can't do this anymore."

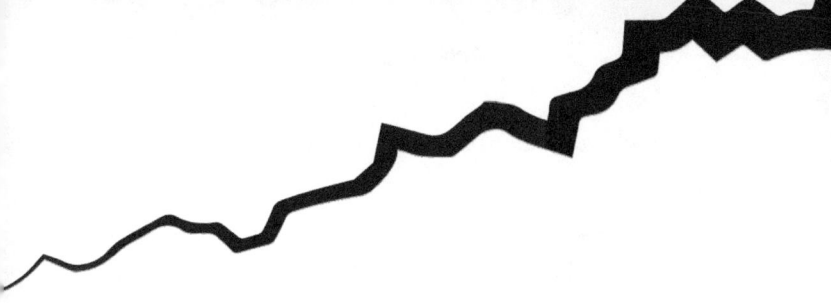

# THIRTY

**"IT WASN'T...**supposed to go like this." Humberto stared at his former colleague lying on the ground. "It... I don't... I shouldn't have—"

Recognizing the shock of a first kill, Evander slowly made his way to the driver's side. "Easy, *amigo*." He reached in nice and easy, and pulled the gun away.

Zoey used the truck's rear tire to stand back up, then placed a hand on the back of her head. "Aaaagh." She winced. "That'll leave a bruise."

Ev holstered his gun before slipping his arm around her. "Zoey, are you okay?" He placed a gentle hand on her hair, moving it around to check for blood. "That was quite the wallop."

His concern made her smile and say, "Forget the wallop, that kiss back there was—"

"Strictly professional," he countered, avoiding eye contact.

"Suuuure it was, *Romeo*." She winked at him. "Almost

like you haven't kissed someone in a while and had some pent-up—"

"Don't even go there." He tightened his lips together and returned to Humberto in the truck's cab. "Listen, buddy, perfect timing on your existential crisis. But we need to unload that animal back there and send it to a safe facility before we leave."

Humberto placed a hand to his chest, mustering everything he could to remain calm. "I should've gotten out of this sooner. This wasn't supposed to—"

"Choices were made," Ev spat out, considering every second they'd been on this mission brought their side task of the kid closer to possible injury or death. "Now you're here, *own it,* and do better." He spotted a handheld controller in the middle console cupholder and seized it.

Zo gave her partner an offended look. "He just killed someone, give him a minute to breathe."

Heading for the trailer door, Ev went rigid and turned around. "And that death will most likely spark a war we're not ready for." Resuming his sprint, he took a moment to study the gadget. "Going to save that kid will add more fuel to the fire." He pressed a button, and the locks disengaged.

Using the trailer wall to keep herself upright, Zo came to the opening and gasped.

Bound to the floor, the creature could barely budge.

Intimidating incisors demanded everyone's attention.

*RROOOOOOAAAAAARR!*

Being in the creature's line of sight, Ev froze. "Saber-tooth."

♀ Smilodon
"Saber-Tooth Tiger"

1.5 m

2.4 m

Zo stepped back a tad, giving the nine-hundred-pound cat some space. "That's the biggest smilodon I've ever seen. SauraCorps recently caught wind of a saber-tooth operation. Bet you this is probably part of—"

"*Don't* get close to this one," Humberto joined them in viewing the feline. "We've had to keep this one tranquilized, it's already taken out three guys."

Pulling out his cellphone, Ev's cautious stare switched to a conniving grin. "Maybe we should let it loose on the rest of your old friends."

Up on the ramp, Zo took slow steps toward the thick-furred saber-tooth. "Oh, you poor, luxurious beauty."

Groaning, the smilodon tried to wrench itself free, but to no avail.

"It's okay," she cooed, getting inside to view the rest of the animal properly. "We're gonna get you back to…."

Blood had stained fur on one of its forearms.

Enraged at the sight of it, she stomped back to the opening. "Hey, who the heck did this?"

Humberto shrugged. "When it attacked, someone pulled out a machete and—"

"Is there a first aid kit in the truck?"

"Zoey, we don't have time for that," Ev advised before going back to his conversation over the phone. "Yeah, hi, this is Evers. We need a Pinpoint extraction for a saber-tooth tiger."

"Screw it." Marching back into the trailer, she took her blue jacket off. "This should hopefully do the trick for you." Hunching to get closer to the injury, she tenderly slipped the piece of clothing around the cat's forearm and flopped the arms together. "Damn, this is gonna hurt."

She cinched it tight.

*RRAAAAAAWR....*

The saber-tooth's shriek echoed out into the open.

Ev took wary steps inside until he'd attached a gadget to the animal's thick coat. "Transponder is operational."

"Is there anything other than the trailer obstructing the animal?" a SauraCorps employee asked on the other end.

"Uh, it's strapped in." Ev backtracked, noting the clips fastened to the floor. "Will that matter?"

"If it remains inside, the beam will curve to meet the transponder. But you'll have to detach the straps first or else it'll take the trailer with it."

Ev's eyes opened wide. "Frig." He crouched and unclipped the first one. "Zo, help me get these off."

Following suit, they'd freed it in less than thirty seconds.

"Done," Ev announced, hustling to make it outside and out of the way. "Ready when you are."

*BLAM-BLAM!*

All three of them cowered and rushed for cover.

Injured, the head chef from the restaurant had staggered outside and fired at them.

*BLAM!*

One of the bullets clipped the transponder, making it fritz.

*ZEEUU-ZEEUU-ZEEUU-BWOOOOM!*

A surging beam of electric-blues and whites descended from the sky, whisking away the prehistoric cat.

"Smilodon's gone, we need to get out of here." Ev returned fire and grabbed Zo's arm, leading her away. He picked up the archaeopteryx carrier on the way and glanced back at Humberto. "Hey, come with us!"

Dumbfounded and without any other option, Humberto hurried after them.

Running out of ammo, the chef tossed the gun back into his apron's pocket and grabbed his phone. Scrolling through his contacts, he connected a call.

He stared out at Alvaro's dead body. "El Cazador, you won't believe what just happened here."

Making it back to the car, Ev's phone rang as he plopped the carrier in the back seat. He answered it while hopping in the front. "Hello? Yeah, I placed the transponder on the—what do you mean 'it didn't show up'? I did exactly like you told me."

Zo clicked her seatbelt in before checking on the frightened archaeopteryx pair. "The saber-tooth didn't arrive at HQ?"

Situating himself in the back passenger seat, Humberto didn't know what to do or say about anything. He'd just taken out Alvaro, and an ethereal teleportation beam had flashed down before his eyes. Among everything, only one thing dominated his full attention. *I need to make sure my kids are safe.*

"Well, it's not here, we saw it teleport," Evander responded to the SauraCorps personnel. "Can't talk now, we gotta go save some Zavier Sanchez kid."

The name snapped Humberto back to the car. "Did… you just say '*Zavier Sanchez*'?"

Zoey glanced over her shoulder. "Why, you know him?"

Humberto went completely numb. "He's my son."

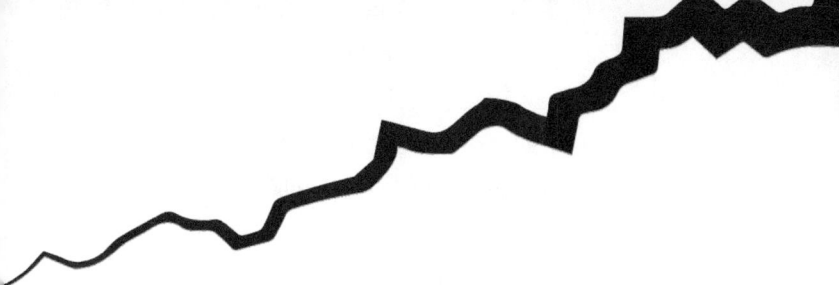

# THIRTY-ONE

**"GONNA BURN** a hole right through this deck, missy." Earnest plucked herbs from some of the pots by the back door. "Those people are professionals. I'm sure they know what they're doing."

Pacing every six feet or so, Lucero had entered a dark place in her mind. "What if they don't get to Zav in time?"

He broke a rosemary stem off a plant and sniffed it for its comforting aroma. "Why don't you come on in and help me make supper."

Taking a pause, she unfolded her arms to throw her hands in the air. "How are you not as worried about this?"

Closing his eyes and pressing his lips together, he drew in a deep breath. "This ain't denial about the situation. This is me keeping busy because there's nothing I or even *you* can do about it right now."

Unable to make a rebuttal, she stood in silent protest.

"All I'm saying is, you can pace or stand there and stew in

your feelings if you want to," he added, hoping his tough love wouldn't turn her against him. "But the longer you stew about it, despair is gonna eat that stew right up." He snapped a sprig of thyme from its pot and thumbed through the collection of herbs in his palm. "As for me, I'd rather eat some stew than worry about what I can't control."

Luz let his words in, even though part of her didn't want to listen. She'd already lost her mom to cancer. *I can't lose Zavier, too.* Subconsciously, her hands hung at her sides and balled into fists. *And Dad is wrapped up in a cartel, he might as well be....*

Giving her one last glance, Earnie opted to leave her to her thoughts. Stepping through the doorway, he shuffled a half-step. "Luz, if you don't mind at least grabbing some—"

Gone.

Hearing footsteps in the gravel, he turned around fully.

She sprinted toward the barn.

Nodding to himself, he didn't say another word as he closed the door behind him.

As soon as Luz made it inside the large wooden structure, she stumbled to her knees. Her lungs sucked in shuddering breaths, restricting the air from coming back out. A heartbroken wail ripped out of her chest, echoing throughout the barn.

Losing strength in her upper body, she let herself collapse to the dirt.

The same thought repeated itself over and over.

*Everything is falling apart.*

Another sob blew dust away from her mouth.

*Everything…is falling…apa—*

*R-R-R-R-R-R-R-ROOOUUUNGH.*

Curious, Tess brought her head inside the shelter while making a low grumble.

Luz propped herself up with an arm and pulled her folded legs under her. "Oh, Tess, what are you doing in here, girl?"

*GR-R-R-R-R-RUUGH.*

Tess nudged her snout into the gloomy girl.

Giggling, Luz placed both hands on the dinosaur's bottom jaw and proceeded to scratch at the scales. "Did my scream make you all concerned, huh?"

Without being told to curtsy, Tess lowered all the way to the ground and snorted air right into Luz's face.

"Blegh, *thanks* for that." Scrunching her nose, Luz blew the odorous breath back out. "Trying to console me or something?"

Tess swayed her head to the side, getting a better look with her reptilian eye. She leaned the crown of her head toward the human as if to give confirmation.

Sighing, Luz rested her forehead against the tip of the tarbosaurus's snout. "I'm just…dealing with more than I can handle right now." Being in the presence of a living thing that couldn't talk back made her become more vulnerable. "And I know Earnie's there for me, but I feel like I'm…*all alone* with this."

Letting her body slouch forward, she embraced the dinosaur's rough-yet-cool scales.

*KAOW-KAOW-REEAAOOW!*

She pulled her head back as the three austroraptors made

their presence known while entering the rustic barn. "Ah, the three austro-teers for more emotional support."

Aramis—identified by a greenish hue around its eyes and aptly named for its more affectionate nature—slinked over, rubbing its head into hers.

Some of her hair flopped onto Aramis's crown, making her laugh at the ridiculous sight. "That hair color doesn't suit you, might want to go blonde or somethi—"

*GRAAAOOOW-snort-EEAAOOGH!*

Gladys the glyptodon scuttled in, joining the unconventional herd. She trudged up to her human friend, tucked her feet in, and dropped her oversized shell to the ground.

"What is all this?" Luz laughed at the bizarre happenings. "Are you all vying for the position as my emotional support pet?"

Even Peggy the parasaurolophus popped her head in and honked.

"Okay, okay, I get it," Luz hollered, sensing an instinctual form of care from all of the prehistoric creatures. Considering the fair amount of time she'd spent with each and every one of them, she truly appreciated each bond she'd formed with them all. Glancing around at the animals, she reminded herself, *Pets do become part of the family.* Still petting Tess, she rested her cheek against the scaley hide. "Guess I'm not alone after all."

Standing back up and kissing the top of Tess's snout, she managed a smile. "Mom would've loved all of you."

# THIRTY-TWO

**"A BLOB...** of toothpaste... is called a nurdle," Zavier spit out, still strapped to the chair, keeping his eyes closed, and heaving for breaths of air. A bruise had started to form on his left eye, and his cheek stung. He figured he'd been there for an hour or so, though it felt like an eternity.

*Smack!*

Blanca's hand made contact with his face again.

Flexing her fingers, she rubbed her open palm for relief. "Still with the useless facts? It's been almost an hour."

Letting his head hang back, Zav managed a single chuckle. "Just...don't ask me...what I had for breakfast... yesterday."

Winding up a fist, she stopped and roared in frustration. "Forget it." She walked past him. "I can't deal with you anymore."

He groaned in reply, "Oh, thank Go—"

Blanca grabbed the chair, leaned it back, and began

dragging it.

"Wait, what are you do—"

"Desperate measures." She pulled out a ring of keys as she neared one of the cages. "Meet your new cellmate." Propping him up beside a door made of bars, she slipped a key into a heavy-duty padlock.

"Screw that!" Realizing where she'd brought him to, he rocked back and forth, making the chair fall sideways. "It'll kill me!"

Dragging the chair inside, she propped him back up. Slicing through the zip-ties, she left the last one intact and brought her lips to his ear. "Funny, you weren't afraid to die an hour ago."

Thrust forward, he sprawled onto the cold metal. "No... but...I—"

*Clang!*

"Fun fact..." She spoke with a devious smile. "...woolly rhinos are extremely territorial, and their horns can be as tall as the average man."

Zav scrambled to his feet and stared straight ahead.

*BRRAAAAUUUUGH!*

Right across from him, the two-ton rhino pounded a foot into the floor and snorted.

He backed into the metal bar wall and plastered himself against it. "If you know my dad, and he finds out you let me die—"

"Newcomers in the group usually don't *last long,* anyway," she countered without a speck of bother. "Give me something *useful* for once, and no one has to know any of this happened."

"Coming up on the location." Zoey studied the pinpoint on her phone's map. "Almost right on top of it."

Sighting the warehouse across the road, Evander pulled over, leaving a decent space to survey the environment. "Is that the one, 'Berto?"

Humberto didn't even respond. Countless regrets swarmed his mind like wasps, stinging and biting him without letup. *Zavier...* He prayed and wished for a miracle. *...please be ali—*

"Humberto, snap out of it," Evander barked back, mindful of timing. "Is this the place?"

Jarred out of his misery, Humberto peered through the car windows. "*Sí,* this is one of the stock locations." Placing his hand on the handle, he noticed a vehicle just beyond the building. "*Blanca,* she's in there."

"Sounds like she's not to be messed with," Zo remarked, psyching herself up for another altercation.

Humberto made a single uneasy chuckle. "Exactly."

Ev inserted another mag of bullets into his gun. "Gonna sit this one out, Zo?" He grimaced as he stretched out his injured shoulder. "After what happened earlier, I wouldn't blame you if—"

"My mom didn't sit out her last mission," she responded with determination. "Now what's our game plan, Cupcake?"

"Don't call me that."

"I swear, the spinosaurus—"

*WHA-BANG!*

The woolly rhino slammed its horn into the bars, shaking the entire cage.

Zav had leapt out of the way, only to have to ready himself for another charge. "It broke out on its own!"

Blanca had crossed her arms and simply watched. "And no one else in your neighborhood saw it? It would've left some kind of trail."

"Listen, lady, how do you expect me to know—*frig!*" He dove to the right, avoiding the massive horn. "*Hijo de—*"

*BRRAAAAUUUUGH!*

The rhino flicked its ears, snorting as it repositioned.

"You can't run forever," Blanca remarked in a chill manner. "But you can end this tag session by giving me proper intel."

With his back to Blanca, Zav stared back at the prehistoric animal. He could already sense his legs getting wobbly. Turning around, he grabbed onto the bars and glared straight into her eyes. "Tell my family…that I love—"

"Blanca?"

Both of them looked over to find a familiar face approaching.

"Humberto?"

"Dad!"

As soon as Humberto identified his son inside the cage,

he bared his teeth. "Blanca! How could you…. *Why?* Why is he *in there?*"

She unsheathed her knife, keeping it behind her back for now. "Because he did something with that spinosaurus, and I'd like to know—"

"She tased and kidnapped me, Dad!" Zav shouted before ducking to the floor as the rhino made a dent in the bars. "Get me *out of*—"

"Your son is *lying* to you. He lied about the spinosaurus, too." Blanca only had a couple more feet to go before reaching Humberto. "And in this business, well…" She waved a hand in Zav's direction. "…this is what happens to liars and thieves."

Locking eyes with his exhausted son, Humberto wanted to bare his teeth at Blanca. "Let him out *now.*" He forced himself to stay composed. "There's no need for this."

She scrunched her nose while shaking her head. "Yeah… no. See, that spinosaurus entered this warehouse." She revealed the knife, swinging it around to help make threatening gestures. "*My warehouse*—which means part of that cut was supposed to be *mine.*"

Two feet away from him, she glanced down at the reflection in the blade.

Evander had been creeping up from behind.

*WHA-BANG!*

Zav avoided the woolly rhino by a hair, then threw himself at its hide and grabbed on.

Blanca dove between two cages.

With all the creatures around, Ev figured to keep his shot

attempts to a minimum. "*Humberto,* save your kid! We've got Blanca."

Coming out the other side of the cages, Blanca headed for a stash of weapons.

*BA-DUM-CRASH!*

Zoey had launched herself off a pile of crates, knocking the cartel member to the concrete floor.

The knife flew out of Blanca's hand, skidding away.

Coming to the cage door, Humberto stared at the padlock. "Zav! I'm so sorry, this…. This should have *never* happened…" He found his son up on top of the rhino. "…to…you?"

Settling onto the cage floor, the submissive rhino made a delighted groan.

"Should've thought…of this before." Straddling the animal's neck, an out-of-breath Zav used both hands to scratch all over its head and behind the ears. "Thankfully… every animal…loves scritches."

Back on their feet, Zo and Blanca exchanged punches and kicks.

Zo protected her head with her left elbow, taking a blow and reaching out to snag her enemy's hair.

Blanca retracted her arms to her chest, absorbing Zo's knee and wrapping her hands around the lower leg. Engaging her core, she heaved the leg upward.

Falling backward, Zo smacked into the floor.

Also going down, Blanca shrieked as strands of hair tore out of her head. She reached out to reclaim her knife and lifted it above Zo's head.

*BLAM-BLAM!*

One of Ev's bullets knocked the knife out of her hand again.

Smirking, Zo fed the base of her palm to Blanca's chin and shoved her off. Scrambling to get back up, she gave a grateful glance to Ev. "I totally had her."

He kept his gun trained on the cartel member. "You're welcome."

Blanca wiped blood from her mouth as she struggled to stand. "If my father finds out that this place is compromised, or that you killed me, there will be nowhere you can run or hide."

Ev acknowledged the information with a grunt. "Noted."

*BLAM-CRACK!*

Blanca's left knee shattered.

A hollow burn replaced all strength in her leg as she collapsed and wailed.

"Really?" Zo gave him an unimpressed stare. "The knee, *again?*"

"What?" He advanced toward Blanca, pulling handcuffs out of his back pocket. "There's something so *satisfying* about a good kneecapping."

Humberto came around the cage to find his ex-coworker apprehended. "Her keys, grab her keys. I need them for Zavier."

After Ev cuffed Blanca, he searched and located the keys and tossed them over.

Off to the side, Zo loosened up and cataloged sore spots on her body. The physical injuries received from Alvaro and Blanca had put her in a weakened state. Taking in the warehouse and the creatures imprisoned within it made her tear up. "We're getting these animals out of here, too, right?"

Ev admired Blanca's knife and made his belt its new home. "Uh, I don't think I have enough transponders for all of them. Call it in."

Humberto finally found the right key and disengaged the padlock. "Come on out, Zav, you're safe now. We have…" He hesitated, knowing their impending conversation wouldn't be an easy one. "…a lot to talk about."

Zav hopped off the rhino and patted it on the cheek. "But Dad, can we keep Rory?"

"Rory?"

"Actually, one sec." Zav crouched and checked the rhino. "Yep, Rory's a boy."

With her phone to her ear, Zo leaned against the rhino's cage. "Hey, Seb. We just took control of one of the cartel's warehouses, and we've got a lot of animals that need relocating."

"We'll send a crew over right away," Sebastian responded. "Need anything else?"

"A spicy calzone with extra marinara." Zoey didn't miss a beat. "Want anything, Ev?"

"If we're going Italian, sausage and fennel pizza." Evander rubbed his shoulder and added, "And get them to send a medic."

# THIRTY-THREE

**"YOU'VE KNEECAPPED** three people in the last two days." Having teleported there within a few minutes thanks to Project Pinpoint, Sebastian stood among his friends while his other employees hustled around the warehouse. "And there was no other way of apprehending her?"

As a paramedic inspected her for a concussion, Zoey smirked while dabbing a final piece of calzone in marinara. "I had her on the ropes."

Evander grunted while chewing on a piece of his pizza. "The woman assaulted, kidnapped, and tried to turn the kid into a smear on the ground." He winced as another paramedic removed the bullet from his shoulder. "Blowing her knee to bits was the least I could do."

"I admire your efficiency." Seb pinched the bridge of his nose. "But I need you to find a better option."

Zo and Ev exchanged glances and snickered.

Seb picked up on it and frowned. "I don't see the humor

in—"

*"Kneed?"* Zo chuckled, pointing at her bending knee.

Ev burst out laughing before savoring another bite of pizza. "Beat me to it. Oh, before I forget, there's some archaeopteryx in the back seat of my Benz."

Zo snickered to herself. "Yeah, I'm slowly changing him. He allows food and animals on Betty's upholstery now."

Rubbing a palm against his face, Seb sighed. "I see my pairing of you two has created an…*interesting* dynamic."

With a cheeky grin, Zo finished her calzone. "Oh, we were the *dynamic* duo earlier—"

"Shut it." Flushed in his cheeks, Ev shot a glare at her. "They would've started shooting if we didn't confuse them first."

Seb squinted. "Am I missing somethi—"

"Nope." Ev licked pizza oil off a finger. "Just a purely professional pressing of lips together."

"Whoa, what—*really?*" Seb immediately turned to look at Zoey. "You two?" He couldn't stop glancing back and forth at them. "You two *kissed?*"

Zo stared at Ev in amusement. "At least *Seb* knows what to call it. Don't have to sound so formal about it, Jellybean."

Meanwhile, near the front of the warehouse, Humberto and Zavier had begun their complex heart-to-heart.

"So…" Zav crossed his arms. "…a cartel, huh?"

Humberto stared at the floor, his face covered in shame. "I

don't…." So many things came to mind of how to respond, but only one thing came out. "I don't know where to start."

"Are we struggling for money?" Zav stepped forward, trying to meet his father's gaze. "Because I could've always picked up extra shifts, or—"

"After your mother died, I…." Every breath he took burned his lungs with remorse. As his legs weakened, he lowered himself onto a small crate. "As you and your sister could probably tell, I spiraled into a very dark place."

Zav grimaced and nodded. "We all did."

"And with her loss, I lost a huge part of who I was." Humberto spoke with a heaviness in his tone, as if every regret had collapsed onto him like a mountain. Lifting his watery eyes to take in the warehouse and the chaos he'd been a part of, he scratched at his tightening neck. "Clearly, all of this was not the way to try and find it again, even if money kept coming in. But you and Luz…neither of you have ever given me a day of grief, and I go getting myself into this mess. I should've gotten out of it earlier, and I'm *so stupid* for getting deeper into it, and when I heard you were taken, I—"

"*Dad.*" Zav let his arms uncross to grasp his father's shoulders. "I'm still alive, and I'm right here. Luz and I have *always* been right here."

"But Blanca could've killed—"

"You joined a cartel without thinking straight," Zav countered, placing a hand on the side of his dad's face. "That Blanca lady chose to do what she did with a clear head." He sat down beside him. "I mean, yeah, my head feels like it played a million rounds of *Whack-A-Mole*, and I'm pretty sure all my pairs of pants smell like pee now."

Humberto let a chuckle slip out as he patted his son's leg.

"But I was ready to *die* for you and Luz."

Their eyes finally met.

Humberto opted to not tell his son about killing Alvaro, though he'd done so to protect his family and those who reminded him about doing the right thing. "I love you, son."

"Back at you, Dad."

Two SauraCorps guards stood by an apprehended Blanca. Neither of them took their eyes off of her.

Zip-tied to a chair, Blanca observed Sebastian, Evander, and Zoey off to her left. In livid silence, she grimaced as her blown knee sent excruciating spasms throughout her leg.

A pair of stegosauruses she'd agreed to send to buyers were examined and documented. Over in another corner, a SauraCorps member tried to handle juvenile pteranodons, which had already been paid for. Every single creature she'd currently collected and organized multi-million-dollar deals for had been prepped for transport.

Flexing her fingers, she scowled at the SauraCorps infestation.

Her phone started ringing.

Seb, Ev, and Zo all swung a collective gaze to her.

"One of you will want to get that," Blanca suggested. "He

doesn't like to call twice."

Taking charge, Sebastian marched over and pulled her phone out. Only a phone number with no name showed on the screen. Two ominous rings later, he accepted it.

A man on the other end spoke Spanish at a furious pace.

Sebastian eventually revealed himself. "If you're looking for Blanca, she's currently indisposed."

Still furious, the man spit back, "Who is this?"

After clearing his throat, Sebastian went on, "This is SauraCorps, and who am I speaking to right no—"

"Is she alive?"

Sebastian glanced over at her and tensed his jaw. "I don't know who you're—"

"My daughter Blanca, is she still alive?"

Taking the phone away from his ear, Sebastian covered the mic with his hand. "Wait, you wouldn't happen to be *El Cazador's* daughter, would you?"

Blanca revealed a cunning grin.

Eyes wide open, Zo covered her mouth. "Ev, you just shot the cartel leader's daughter?"

"Frig." Ev rushed right over and whispered, "Put it on speaker."

Doing so, Sebastian returned to the call. "I can guarantee you she's still alive, one second." He held the cellphone out to Blanca. "Go ahead."

"*Hola, Padre.*" She spoke in a sly, mischievous fashion. "I'm okay, I still have *one working leg* to—"

"Gag her!" Ev instructed the guards, grabbing the phone to cover its mic and distort their voices. "Seb, we've just

bashed our foot into a wasp's nest we weren't prepared for."
With intensity in his eyes, he glanced at Zo coming up
beside him. "Alvaro has already been taken out. If we try to
use Blanca for leverage, it'll make things way worse."

Zo placed her hands on her hips. "We could set a trap."

"Do we have anything in play to offer him?" Sebastian
could hear the cartel chief muttering something inaudible.
"His pockets are deep, and his forces are exceptional."

Side by side, the Sanchez men returned to the group.

When Humberto noticed everyone's troubled faces, he
immediately became uneasy. "What's happening?"

"To whoever is listening…" El Cazador raised his
commanding voice. "…one of my men informed me earlier
that Alvaro Balderas was killed by Humberto Sanchez."

Zavier looked to his father, whose face had hardened
with embarrassment. "Dad? You…*killed* someo—"

"I've also been informed he has a daughter as well," El
Cazador added. "Lucero, *Sí?*"

Tension intensified among everyone in the vicinity of the
phone.

Infuriated beyond reason, Humberto charged forward.
"If you touch a *single hair* on her head—"

"Let my daughter free." El Cazador's ultimatum came
out calm and devious. "Take your precious animals, but let
Blanca walk, and Lucero Sanchez will be left alone."

Zo stared at the phone. "He could be bluffing."

Ev handed the phone over to his superior. "It's your call."

Sebastian took the phone and closed his eyes. "Remove
her handcuffs."

Everyone watched as the SauraCorps guards released Blanca.

No one said a word as she stood up and favored her injured leg.

She shifted between smirking and flinching in pain. Repossessing her phone, she winked. "Pleasure...doing *business*...with SauraCorps."

# THIRTY-FOUR

**WITHIN FIVE** minutes of Blanca's departure, the warehouse buzzed with SauraCorps employees and operatives.

"Gotta work double-time now. Hustle, hustle!" Evander clapped his hands to get the attention of as many as possible. On high alert, his mind ran through potential situations. "We've got a lot to cover before we finish up here."

Zoey twisted back and forth, loosening up her back. "Do you think they're watching us right now?"

"Wouldn't doubt it." Ev checked every inner corner of the warehouse. "Don't see any cameras in here. Doesn't mean there aren't any, though."

Sebastian addressed the Sanchez men. "Considering El Cazador knows you killed Alvaro, and who you and your family are, you won't be safe going back to your home."

Humberto shook his head, which morphed into a nod. "You're right." He looked to his son, concerned once again for his family's wellbeing. "There's...nowhere we can go."

Beside his dad, Zavier pulled out his phone, which SauraCorps had retrieved from Blanca earlier. "Do you think they know where Luz is?"

Ev piped up. "Possibly. Cazador could've been bluffing, though."

Sebastian added, "Bluff or not, I wasn't going to risk a kid's life."

One of the SauraCorps employees wheeled a cage over with them. "Sir, figured you'd want to see this."

Giving the creature a closer look, he recognized the species. "*Pulmonoscorpious.* I haven't seen one of these in a whi—"

An order form for the dog-sized scorpion met his hands.

"*The Bug Collector?*" His eyes lit up, taken by complete surprise. "This…. Wow, okay, notify our task force back at HQ that we have a lead."

Another of SauraCorps' personnel approached. "Some young girl is at the front asking about… It's Zavier, right?"

Confused, Zav started for the entrance. "Can't be Luz, she's at Earnie's ranch." Getting closer, he spied a friendly face beyond another SauraCorps guard. "Daira?"

"Zav, you're *alive!*" she screamed with a baseball bat in hand, blowing past the man to give Zav a solid hug. "I followed that crazy chick here. Then I saw the other people come in, and then that chick left, and I didn't know—"

"You…followed us all the way here?" He hugged her back, while realizing she'd risked her life to go after Blanca. "Daira, you didn't have to—"

"Of course I did, you're my bestie's brother," she

countered, tightening her embrace. "And, well…you're like a bro to me, too."

He finally noticed the wooden sports club. "Uh, why the baseball bat?"

"Oh, right." She slapped the bat into her free hand twice. "It's for safety reasons, and if I had the opportunity to mess up that woman's head."

He snort-laughed. "Damn, Daira, I didn't realize you were that feisty."

"So what is all this?" She peeked around, getting more curious the more she stood there. "Is this some kind of covert operation or somethi—hold on, are those…*dinosaurs* back there?"

"It's, uh…." He figured the SauraCorps personnel would appreciate some secrecy. "Actually, I don't think I can really talk about it. Though, I think Dad and I might have to go into hiding or something."

"Hiding from who?" Daira took a step back. "From that woman? Hold up, is this…*cartel*-level stuff?"

"Daira, thank you for everything." He placed a hand on her shoulder. "But you should probably go home, for your safety."

"That settles it, then." Sebastian turned to address Humberto, having come to an agreement on a plan of action. "Ev and Zo will help you and your son find a place to stay. I'll foot the bill on wherever you end up."

After everything Humberto had gone through, he struggled to smile. "Thank you for your kindness, sir."

"No problem at all." Sebastian then tapped Ev on the arm. "Make sure it's as close to you as possible to keep them protected."

Ev nodded. "Affirmative."

Zo raised an eyebrow. "Maybe something's opened up at our hotel."

He made an amused grunt. "Doubt it, *bro.*"

Sebastian squinted, still trying to figure out more of the dynamic between Ev and Zo. "Unfortunately, I have to deal with something tonight. But maybe we could all meet up at Mr. Pardy's ranch tomorrow morning. Sound like a plan?"

"Which reminds me…" Ev selected a past caller on his phone and pressed a button. "…should probably let them know Zavier is okay." He waited while the generic ringing sang its tune.

The person on the other end started with, "Ol' Earnie here in your ear."

"Earnest, this is Evander, the man you contacted earlier about the kidnapping," Ev answered in a professional tone. "He's a little banged up, but he's alive."

"Oh, thank the Lord Almighty in the heavens," Earnie responded in a jovial and appreciative manner. "And thank you, uh, Mr. Evander. His sister will be relieved to hear that, if I can find her, that is."

Ev pursed his lips. "She's *missing?*"

"No, no, not like that." Earnie chuckled. "She's out on the ranch somewhere. Saw her take Tess out for another ride."

Recalling the tarbosaurus, Ev cleared his throat. "Speaking about the ranch, you said you'd be open to talking if we saved the kid."

Earnie groaned. "And I'm a man of my word." An incessant beeping came from the background, and he turned it off. "Sorry, 'bout that, my stew's ready. Uh, when were you thinking of getting together, then?"

"How's tomorrow morning, say around oh-nine-hundred?"

"Just say nine, army boy," Earnie responded, followed by a tsk. "Don't have much *time* left on this earth, so don't take up more than you need to."

Snort-laughing, Evander remarked, "Roger that, Mr. Pardy."

# THIRTY-FIVE

**EL CAZADOR** stood on the second-floor balcony of his mansion. Holding a drink in one hand, he clutched his phone in the other. "Is anyone following you, *mija?*"

On her way back, Blanca slammed her hand into the steering wheel. "My crew should've been with me. I was so stupid—"

"Blanca, are you being *followed?*"

She checked her mirrors. "No."

"Good." He repoured his glass from his most expensive tequila bottle, then gazed out at the beginnings of sunset. "I'll have a doctor and a bottle waiting for you."

She sighed and winced after hitting a bump in the road. "Ley Nine-Twenty-Five Diamante?"

"All thirty-five million dollars of it." After shooting back the alcohol, he expelled a manly, satisfied growl. "And if we don't take care of SauraCorps, business won't be so good anymore."

"I had roughly *two billion* worth of assets in that warehouse." Aggravated, she wished she could've spit venom at Sebastian and his men. "And they're in the process of confiscating all of them."

"Don't worry, *mija*." El Cazador took a few steps over to a table and tapped on a tablet. "Certain things have been set in motion."

She drove over a pothole and sucked in a sharp breath. "Something that will help us with SauraCorps?"

"Not exactly," he responded while accessing files of intel. "Once I'd heard Humberto killed Alvaro…" He signed a cross in front of his chest with his free hand, respecting his lieutenant. "…I immediately assigned hackers to access phone systems. We found his daughter's cellphone record and started tracking."

She sped up in excitement. "Did you find her?"

"We have a general area," he answered with pride. "With satellites, we're currently scanning the terrain of her last known position." A topographical map popped up on his tablet. "Somewhere near Big Bend National Park."

"Really?" She tried moving her leg slightly, which made her shriek. "We haaaa-haven't been out there in a long time."

He paused for a moment. "Blanca, since we're talking, my financier has brought to my attention some missing funds."

"My paperwork is spotless," she shot back, getting offended. "And I'm your *daughter*."

"Yes, *mija*, but I have people to pay," he countered, keeping composed. "And if funds are missing and I can't, then I'll have to answer to—"

*Ding!*

A notification popped up, and an indicator dot appeared.

"Oh, we have a location." Spreading his fingers to enlarge the image, he tensed his jaw with determination. Odd shapes scattered about the landscape caught his eye. "Wait, are those what I think…."

Eager to hear, Blanca turned up her vehicle's speakers. "Tell me!"

"These are…." A scheming grin overtook El Cazador. All of the odd shapes became dollar signs in his eyes. "*Dinosaurs.*"

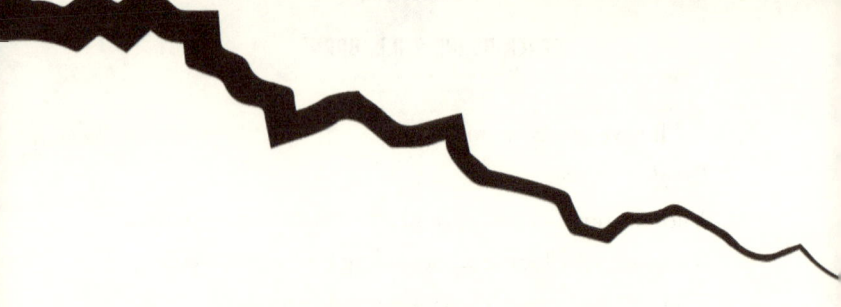

# THIRTY-SIX

**ALMOST TO** the lake on Earnie's property, Lucero allowed Tess to trot at a relaxing pace. Golden hour hues transformed the rocky terrain into more beautiful reds and oranges. The glowing craggy mountains stood out as if they were friends welcoming her back to their home. She inhaled deeply, trying her best to force down her fears.

Tess stopped at the lake's edge and grumbled peacefully.

"Nothing else like it, eh, Tess?" Luz sighed with content as she reached forward to scratch at the leathery scales.

*Ksh-zzt-ksh-zzt-ksh-zzt.*

A crackle came from the long-range walkie-talkie hooked to her belt. She'd taken it from the barn before going on her ride.

Earnie's voice came through. "Luz, you there, girl?"

Unclipping it, she brought it to her mouth. "Any news on Zav?"

"Just heard back that Zav was rescued," he reported with

relief and cheer in his voice. "Him and your pops are safe and sound,"

"Oh, *thank God!*" She placed a hand to her chest. Leaning forward, she allowed herself to release all the tension and dread she'd been holding in. Tears fell from her eyes to the saddle. "And thank you for letting me know, Earnie. I'll give them a call when I get back."

"Stew will be in the fridge waiting for you."

She repositioned her hand to her forehead. "Honestly, today's been so insane, I don't even feel like eating."

Earnie paused for a moment before speaking up again. "Listen, Luz, about what I said earlier, I was simply tryin' to—"

"It's all good," she responded with appreciation. "Like you said, you always treat me like I'm one of your own."

He chuckled. "Always will."

Taking in the stunning remainder of breathtaking sunset, she added, "I may not have wanted to hear it, but I definitely needed to."

With an audible smile, Earnie said, "Enjoy the rest of your ride, lil' missy."

She ended the conversation with, "Thanks, we'll be back soon." Clipping the walkie back onto her waist, she spotted a sail protruding from the water's surface. "Looks like our new friend Solita is coming over."

The spinosaurus' elongated head emerged. Water cascaded off Solita's lean body as she came within a few feet of them.

Luz grinned. "Are you liking things so far, Soli—"

*HI-I-I-I-I-I-I-ISSSSSS!*

*Snap!*

Solita had attempted to nip at the tarbosaurus.

"Whoa, jeez!" Luz squeezed her legs to hold on. "Solita, stop!"

*RRRROOOOOOUUUUUUHH!*

Undeterred by the adolescent spinosaurus, Tess prodded her snout into Solita's neck and growled back.

"What is—*argh*—this?" Luz tightened her grip on the reins. "Some kind of territorial dispute?"

Both of the dinosaurs made the ground tremble as they sparred.

Other creatures within the vicinity either scattered or stared at the formidable show of strength.

Solita snapped her toothy jaws in front of Tess's face. She hissed louder to make them back off and leave.

"Tess has been here *way longer* than you, Solita." Luz clutched the saddle horn with her other hand, hoping she wouldn't become some kind of collateral damage. "At least she's…making herself at home."

After ramming her head into Solita's, Tess used the rest of her powerful body to knock the spinosaurus off-balance and to the ground.

Luz engaged her core, managing to keep herself mostly upright during the quarrel between prehistoric beasts. "Come on, ladies! There's enough ranch for all of—"

*HI-I-I-ISSSS!*

Solita crouched and sprang upward, giving Tess a broad bodycheck.

The force knocked Tess off of her left foot.

"Frig!" Bailing, Luz released the reins and flailed through the air.

A tree branch tore through her shirt.

She screamed while hurtling toward a boulder.

*THWACK!*

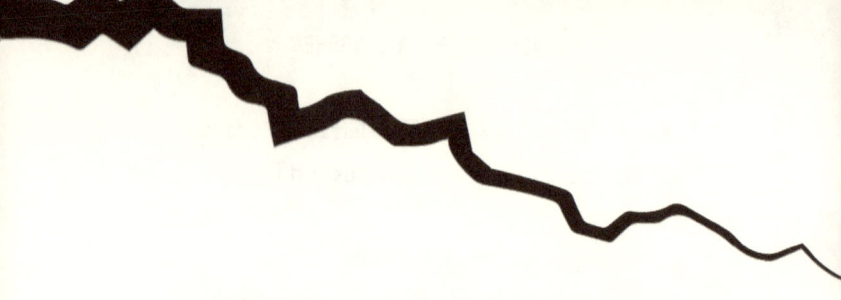

# THIRTY-SEVEN

## SHANGHAI, CHINA

"CODEWORD."

On the outside of the secured door, a bearded man gripped his cane. "Archo…sauro…morpha."

The pair of guards glanced at each other.

One of them nodded, and the other allowed the person inside. "Welcome."

Using the cane for support, the man grinned as he entered.

He found himself among a bigger crowd than he'd anticipated.

Bigwigs, celebrities, and major players in big business all attended, being served finger foods by masked waiters.

One of the servers approached. "Our kentrosaurus kebabs are popular this evening. Care to try one before they're gone?"

The man raised a hand of refusal. "Oh, I just ate. Thank

you, though."

Bowing, the waiter carried on to the other attendees.

"Mr. Bentley!" An Italian came over to shake hands. "Glad you could make it, my friend. They're about to roll out the main event."

"Good to see you, Mr. Franco." Bentley grinned. "I'm excited to see what's available this time."

Franco leaned in and lowered his voice. "I've heard rumors there may be dilophosaurus in the mix." Rubbing his hands together, he bounced his eyebrows up and down. "They don't have frills or spit venom like in the movies, though."

Intrigued, Bentley did some internal math. "My collection doesn't have any of those ye—"

"Welcome, everyone." A masked individual commanded attention from the center of the room. "I hope you've enjoyed the dinosaur hors d'oeuvres so far. If you haven't tried the protoceratops pâté, I highly recommend it."

Bentley whispered to Franco, "Personally, I'm tired of the dino-meat trend."

Glancing around, the secretive host continued. "Tonight, our presentation consists of dinosaurs from Asia. For our loyal patrons, we appreciate your continued loyalty and trustworthiness. You will have your pick of one free asset along with your order."

As he finished his sentence, multiple personnel wheeled in short silver columns.

At the top of each of them, a glass dome protected the contents inside.

Twenty of the apparatuses had been lined up in single file.

With gusto, the host announced, "You may begin."

*PSSSSHHHHT!*

Hydraulics engaged as the glass domes opened.

Clutches of eggs sat in manmade nests. Each housing indicated which dinosaurs were being incubated. Barcodes had been applied to each shell.

The two friends stepped forward, as well as many others.

Bentley took pictures with a specific phone app linked to the function. "Definitely getting a pair of dilophosaurus."

Two incubators down, Franco snapped photos for himself. "Qianzhousaurus and oviraptors are down here if you want any."

Hearing the unique name, Bentley joined his friend. "Sad to think we need to acquire creatures this way now, since adult-sized dinos are easier for SauraCorps to track."

Franco chuckled. "Whoever thought to turn it into a '*save the dinosaurs*' company was a complete idiot." Lowering his face to a collection of udanoceratops eggs, he smirked. "There's more money in taking the dinos, not saving them." In his peripheral, he noticed his English friend inconspicuously dropping something into the incubator. "*Bentley?*"

"Hmm?" Bentley simply smiled. "Oh, is that the udano—"

"What did you just do?" Franco rushed over. "What was that?"

"What was what?" Perplexed, Bentley retreated a step. "I was inspecting—"

"I saw you *drop something* in the nest." Bringing his mouth closer to his friend's ear, Franco whispered, "If you get caught, it will be months until they get this up and running again."

Still grinning, Bentley turned to look him in the eyes. "That's precisely the idea."

*CRASH!*

The front door burst open.

Armed men stormed the room.

Some of the food servers dropped their trays and managed to cart a few incubators out of sight.

"Down on the ground, now!" one of the operatives called out, swinging her rifle back and forth. "Anyone tries to run, and you will be taken down with force."

Pressing a button on a device, the host closed all of the incubators to keep his organization's profitable eggs safe. "And you are all trespassing."

The leading operative marched over, shoved the host into one of the glass domes, and proceeded to handcuff him. "Not when you're illegally selling animals, offspring, and by-products." Finishing up, she noticed Bentley glancing up as he also got detained. Keeping their mole from getting found out by anyone else, she moved on. "This operation is now under the jurisdiction of SauraCorps. You all have the right to remain silent. Anything you all say can and will be used against you in a court of law...."

Once the criminals had been detained, the task force commander returned to a discreet van across the road. Hopping back in, she called her superior. "Mrs. Sharpe, the Shanghai intel was good. Only a small few got away."

"Excellent work, Miss Aponte."

"Managed to even detain some Hollywood people and take pictures with them…in handcuffs, that is."

"As long as they didn't suspect our own actor," Felicia Sharpe remarked, pleased to hear of the successful mission. "Guess Mr. Bentley will have to change his name yet again."

"He dropped a few trackers into the incubators," Aponte brought up as she checked over a colleague's shoulder. Red dots moved among a pair of screens. "We let a couple of them get away, but we'll find their bases of operations soon enough."

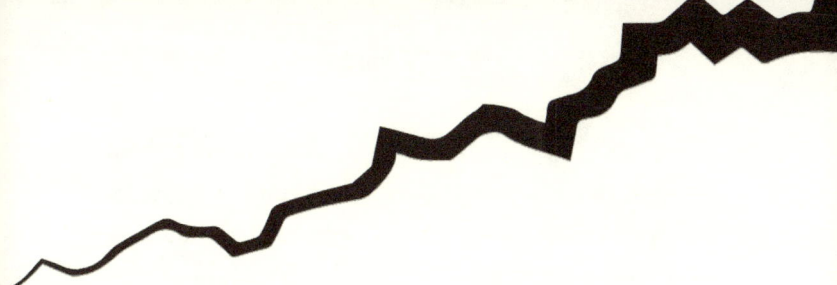

# THIRTY-EIGHT

**BACK AT** their hotel, Evander and Zoey led Humberto and Zavier inside and headed for the front office.

Zav slowed his pace as he finished up a phone call. "Sorry, Yesenia, but I need to raincheck our date. My dad…well… really needs my help with something."

The same young clerk from before greeted Ev and Zo. "Hey, bro and m'lady! Everything all right with your room?"

Once again, Ev grunted with disapproval. "Figured this was a long shot, *Crush,* but would there be an extra room by chance for our friends here?"

Zo gave Ev a surprised stare. "Did you just make a *Finding Nemo* reference?"

"In-flight movies help me sleep sometimes."

"Let me check…." The clerk typed away on the keyboard and clicked the mouse a few times. "Right-right-right, one of the little league kiddos got food poisoning and the fam hightailed it back home. It's got a queen."

"Figures." Ev pulled out his wallet. "We'll take it, and put their tab on mine." He tapped his credit card to the reader and addressed the Sanchez men. "Order whatever you want from room service. You'll both feel better with some food in you."

"Again, thank you." Humberto then patted his son on the shoulder. "Is Luz still not answering her phone?"

Zav hung up again. "That stupid ranch is so spotty. I'll try Earnie, too."

Ev came over and handed them their room keys. "Now, would you both rather be on your own as a family…" He glanced over at Zo. "…or would you like me to join you for protection?"

"Not so fast," Zo put herself between the three of them and addressed her partner. "We have some mission celebrating to do, plus, we should go over our pitch to Earnie for tomorrow."

"Celebrating? What are you—"

"They'll be fine," she grabbed him by the arm and pushed the elevator button. "Question: have you ever tried *biska?*"

Entering their hotel room, Zo immediately rushed over to her duffle bag. "Thankfully when Seb sent guys back to Croatia, they returned with my free bottle of biska."

Ev tossed his jacket onto the king-sized bed. "Those Sanchez guys just went through a traumatic experience." After locking the door, he popped his head in the bathroom to check for possible cartel members hiding in wait. "They've got targets on their back now."

"Would you rather all four of us hunker down in here?" She pulled out the bottle of mistletoe brandy. "We're already heading toward the 'one-bed trope.'"

"Excuse me?"

She uncorked the liquor and waved the cork around. "Ev, look me in the eyes and tell me you didn't feel *something* when we kissed in the kitchen."

He tensed. "It was part of the job."

She scoffed. "I don't believe you."

"Believe it," he rebutted with a raised voice. "And *drop it,* Zo."

"Look, I've done the whole 'fake-kiss to throw people off' before," she remarked, holding out the biska for him to try. "And in comparison, yours had a little extra *zhuzh* to it."

Ev grabbed the bottle more forcefully than intended and took a swig. Giving it back, he stuck his tongue out with uncertainty. "Not the worst thing I've ever had."

"Stalling and denial, huh?" Zo wore a playful smirk. "Typical."

"I'm asking you nicely…" He sat on the opposite side of the bed from her. "…please, just let it go."

"Really?" She set the bottle down on the hotel room's desk harder than anticipated. "I was about to have a frigging *panic attack* in your car and you still forced my trauma out of me." Bringing her face beside his, she mimicked one of his grunts. "And my name's not *Elsa,* so I won't be *letting this go* anytime soo—"

"She...*left me.*"

Zo could only blink in reply.

Covering his mouth with both hands, he implemented his box-breathing strategy to keep his anxious thoughts from overtaking him. Still, a single tear trickled down his cheek.

"Crap." She flinched her hand a couple of times before letting it rest on his back. "You'd been with someone. No wonder you kept avoiding the subject."

He stared at the wall, fixating on a chip in the paint. "*Two years* of marriage...apparently means *nothing*...when you come home *messed up* from war." He dropped a hand to the bed and scrunched up the duvet, then patted it flat. "I thought Thalia and I would conquer everything together, but my PTSD was the dealbreaker for her."

Wanting to say something, she couldn't bring herself to say anything. No funny quip, no motivational speech. *All he needs is someone to listen.*

He exhaled and clenched his jaw, which helped him maintain a calm demeanor. "I was messed up then, and... because of her giving up on me, I'll admit, I still kind of am."

"No." Zo softened her voice, letting compassion take over. "When we lose the people we love—friends, family, whoever for whatever—grief and PTSD are *never* something to be ashamed of." She removed her hand from his warm back. "We should never be embarrassed or made to feel less of ourselves for working through our traumas." She looked upward at the speckled ceiling. "At least, that's what my therapist tells me."

He recalled nothing about therapy in her personnel file. "Do you still go?"

"Not as much," she answered, stretching her tense neck out. "The way I see it, when we're going through our worst days…" She placed her hand on top of his and squeezed it. "…it's those who stick around that we need to hold on to the hardest."

He lingered on her empathetic sign of friendship. When they had first met, he'd never thought they'd be having heart-to-hearts at all. But learning each other's history and going through peculiar situations together gave him a whole new appreciation for her. "We all have breakdowns. Mine used to be uglier than the one you had yesterday."

Not giving him any eye contact, she sniffled and sighed. "At least you've learned how to keep it together."

He gave a positive grunt. "It took me almost a year to accept that it's okay to *not be* okay." He shifted on the bed to try and connect with her. "When you broke down—and I know I probably came across as insensitive—but do you know what I saw?"

She simply shook her head.

"I saw someone who loved their mom so much that it hurt."

A shaky breath came out of Zo.

"You mentioned shame," Ev continued. "Don't ever be ashamed about having *that much love* for your mom."

Releasing a tense breath, she finally turned her tear-covered face toward him. An endearing smile emerged as her heart broke once more, but found a spot for his kind words to sink in. "This might sound crazy, but I think Seb pairing us together was a good thing."

"Funny, I was just thinking the same."

Zoey chuckled. "Or…it's probably just the biska talking."

Evander nudged his shoulder into hers. "Your mom would be proud of you."

"Earnie's not answering his cell, must be dead or something." Wanting to throw his phone at the wall, Zav chose to keep pacing. "And I don't think he has a landline. Luz mentioned something a while back about him being fed up with telemarketers or something."

Waiting for room service to arrive, an exhausted Humberto laid on the bed and stewed in his thoughts. Hoping to distract himself, he picked up the TV remote and flipped through channels. "Come and sit down, *mijo.*"

Continuing his march from the window to the peephole in the door, Zav checked it once more. "After the day I've had, I'd rather keep an eye out."

Humberto snorted. "After Blanca and running from that woolly rhino, I'm surprised you still have energy left."

"But now Luz could be in trouble!" Zav threw his arms up. "She spends so much freaking time at Earnie's with those dinos, and now that—"

"Dinos?" Humberto sat up straighter. "What do you mean, dinos?"

Zav let his arms slap against his sides. "*Crap.*"

Sliding off the bed, Humberto stepped closer to his son. "You mean...dinosaurs? Are there *actual dinosaurs* on Earnie's ranch?"

Kicking himself internally, Zav dug his fingernails into his palms. "I...wasn't supposed to say anything."

Humberto dropped back onto the bed. His mouth opened, waiting for words to come out. Pieces started connecting together in his mind. "Did you two.... The spinosaurus?"

Buzzing with discomfort, Zav nodded. "Luz and I took it."

"You *lied* to me?"

"Only about that, I swear to—"

"Zavier, how could...." Humberto sifted his hands into his curly hair. "Do you know what they would've done if they'd found out *my own kids* stole the spinosaurus?"

Getting his back up, Zav rubbed the side of his face. "Probably a lot worse than what Blanca got away with."

As exasperation swelled within Humberto, he lifted his hands only to place them on the sides of his son's battered face. His lips trembled as he reined his breathing back to a normal pace. "I swore on your mother's grave that I wouldn't let anything happen to you and Luz. And now...I may have doomed us all."

"Dad." Zavier grabbed onto his father's wrists. "Luz and I still and always will love you, and we'll face whatever happens *together.*"

# THIRTY-NINE

**"THE BULLET** definitely shattered your kneecap," a doctor informed Blanca as they finished applying a brace to her leg. "Even if we tried reconstructive surgery and recovery, you won't be able to move around like you used to."

Off to the side, El Cazador looked at his daughter with disappointment. "Even if she has the best pain meds?"

"Mobility is mobility." The bearded doctor removed his glasses. "Be happy it didn't hit the femoral artery…" He looked back to Blanca. "Or else you could've bled out."

Laid up on a gurney, Blanca tossed back another shot of tequila.

El Cazador pursed his lips. "How about amputation? I know a prosthetic guy who could—"

"We are *not* cutting it off." She whipped her shot glass across the room. "All I need…is to make that man *pay* with his life." She stared at the brace with rage. "We found the girl, we should find the rest of them and take them all out now!"

He rubbed her head and wore a sympathetic grin. "As much as it would please me to hunt them down, we need to stick to the plan."

"And I can *still* be a part of that plan." She swung her legs over the gurney's edge and roared in pain. "*Hijo de la*.... Do we still have...armored vehicles?"

He scrunched his eyebrows together. "*Sí.*"

Blanca's grimace morphed into a sly grin. "Then put me in one of them...and stay out of my way."

El Cazador kissed her on the top of the head. "I will consider it. Rest now, while I go *take care* of a few things."

"If you will give us another chance..." El Cazador spoke to his Cuban contact over the phone. "...then you will have the spinosaurus, plus extra animals for the inconvenience."

"Fine," they answered without hesitation. "We'll meet at the original location."

"*Perfecto. Adiós.*" El Cazador hung up with a triumphant smile, and he pulled a hunting knife from its leather sheath. "So good to know I still have people I can *trust.*" He turned his attention to a built man sitting in a chair. "Wouldn't you say so?"

The man's hands and feet were bound.

His mouth had been gagged with his own sock.

"Some wonder why I named myself El Cazador." Strutting around the trapped man, he admired the shine in the blade. "It's because I have always loved *the hunt.*"

Beads of sweat dripped down the man's brow.

"And I have always admired hunters in the natural world," El Cazador continued, wearing an impressed grin. "Wolves are among the best. A pack of wolves will separate out and surround their prey." Gesturing with the knife in his hand, he brought the tip close to the man's worried face. "Some of them will approach from the rear, and right when the prey starts to look around—"

*Swish-rip!*

El Cazador had slashed through the rope holding the man's right ankle to the chair.

The victim whimpered into the bunched-up sock.

"Then…" El Cazador crouched and placed his free hand on the back of the man's neck. "…other wolves will bite the shoulders and flanks. Sometimes a wolf will go…for the nose."

*Swish-rip!*

He sliced the other restraint around the left ankle.

"Now, *Señor Vidales,* you've worked for me for ten whole years." El Cazador brought his face an inch away from his prisoner. "Word of advice, watch your back more carefully. Because it's come to my attention…" He plucked the sock from his traitor's mouth. "…that *you* told SauraCorps about the Corpus Christi deal at the shipyard."

Vidales spit out dirty sock scum and little fluffs. "I did nothing, I swear to—"

"How much did SauraCorps pay *you* to throw away your loyalty and my trust?"

"Please, it wasn't—"

"And because of *you*—" El Cazador grabbed Vidales's

face. "—my daughter almost *died!*"

*Shhhhiiiing!*

Rope fell from Vidales' wrists.

He'd expected the knife to be plunged into his gut.

El Cazador made his way around the chair, freeing the SauraCorps mole.

Vidales remained still, utterly confused and completely terrified.

"This is yours if you want it." El Cazador handed him a shot glass filled to the brim with tequila. "A farewell drink, if you will."

Staring at the glass, Vidales eventually accepted it and gulped it down.

"Good, good." El Cazador grinned. "Now run."

Internal sirens wailed in Vidales' head. "Run?"

El Cazador's eerie smile didn't waver as he prodded Vidales toward a door with the knife. "Remember those dire wolves from that deal you ruined? Those were originally raised right here on my property."

*AUW-AUW-AUWOOOOOOOOO!*

The distant hair-raising howl echoed toward them.

A menacing chorus of wolves joined in.

Vidales gulped.

"They haven't eaten in almost two weeks." El Cazador shoved him through the door, his smile turning into a maniacal grin. "Enjoy being hunted, *traitor.*"

Among the darkened Texan wilderness, Vidales took the deepest, shakiest breath he'd ever taken.

He glanced back at the door El Cazador had just pushed him through. Outside lights on either side of it flickered off.

*AUWOOOOOOOOO!*

The howl made his entire body go rigid.

As Vidales stepped forward, he strained his eyes as the moon had become his only source of trustworthy light.

Bushes and dry brush rustled off to his left.

A mass of fur dashed behind a boulder.

Vidales took wary steps as he put as much distance as possible between him and El Cazador's mansion.

Making a right, he froze.

Six sets of canine eyes stared at him.

*AUW-AUW-AUWOOOOOOOOO!*

Larger than the others, the alpha dire wolf stood slightly ahead of the others.

Vidales planted his feet.

One by one, the prehistoric wolves broke off from their pack and encircled him. Every movement displayed their swiftness and muscular builds. As they surrounded the man, some yipped while others howled.

Forcing a gulp down his throat, Vidales raised his arms into the air to make himself bigger. "Here we go."

He pressed a finger to his ear. "Kasparek, you read me?"

"We have your location. Cazador took the bait?"

"It got a little *dicey* at some points." Vidales glanced back at the mansion, making sure no one had been watching. "Have you *Pinpointed* the six dire wolves?"

"Locked on and ready."

"Good." Vidales locked eyes with the alpha's. "Let's send them to SauraCorps HQ."

*ZEEEEUUUU-BWOOOOM!*

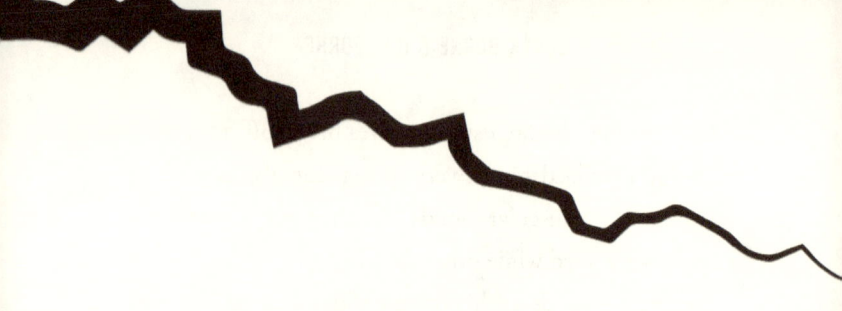

# FORTY

**DIFFUSED DAWN** sunlight beamed onto the hotel bed.

Mouth half-open, Zoey snored herself awake. Laying on her left side, she swished her right arm over the rest of the bed.

No one laid beside her.

Now more awake, she rubbed her face as she sat up to try and find her mission partner. "Ev, where are…."

Evander relaxed in the hotel chair with a small tool in his hands. "Morning, Beaumont."

Her eyes adjusted as she identified his current activity. "Um, are you—"

"Crocheting." Performing a granite stitch, he didn't take his eyes off the pattern. "Therapist recommended it to keep my hands busy. And the hooks could make decent weapons if need be. Plus, never know when you'll need a good scarf."

Zo stared at him for a solid five seconds. "Did you sleep

214

in that chair?"

"All night."

"Ev, you didn't have to."

"Of course I did."

She rubbed her forehead. "Sorry, I can't have a conversation with you while you're doing that. It's just… *weird.*"

Ev paused crocheting for a moment to look at her. "It calms me."

"Uh-huh." Squinting at him, she continued, "Is it because you thought I'd try to snuggle with you?"

"Nope."

"Did I take your preferred side of the bed, or—"

"Because I *respect* you," he answered, honest and firm in his delivery. "Zoey, you are a complex woman who had a bit too much to drink last night." He returned to his soothing pastime. "And this job doesn't allow me to get involved with complex."

Insulted, she pointed at his hands. "You and crocheting is too complex for my brain."

He chuckled. "Get yourself ready. We're grabbing breakfast with the Sanchezes on the way to the ranch."

Half an hour later, Humberto exited the elevator and marched straight over to Ev. "Mr. Evers, something isn't right. Since last night, we haven't been able to make any contact with my daughter. Perhaps we should skip breakfast and head straight there."

Ev flicked his keycard between his fingers. "Let's not jump to any dire conclusions. Didn't you say she's in a bad service spot?"

A sleep-deprived Zavier had lost count of the number of times he'd attempted calls. "But even when I get multiple rings, it goes straight to voicemail. I even tried Earnie, but you know old people and phones."

Over by the doors, Zo urged them on. "Maybe she dropped her phone while riding that tarbosaurus."

On his way out, Humberto gave her a double take. "Tarbosaurus?"

A hesitant Zav exited the hotel. "Yeah, uh…about those horse-riding lessons—"

"Talk about it in the car." Zo placed a hand on her growling stomach as she headed straight for Ev's Mercedes-Benz. "My hangry beast is about to roar like a dino."

Getting situated and comfortable, the group of four headed for the nearest drive-thru.

In the backseat, Humberto couldn't stop fidgeting and rubbed his face. "So not only has she been spending time with these creatures, she's learned how to *ride them,* too?"

Zav placed a sincere hand to his chest. "To be fair, I didn't really know she was riding them. That's new to me."

In the front passenger seat, Zo glanced back at them. "She scared us off the ranch while up on the tarbosaurus." Recalling the events, she chuckled through her nose. "Named it Tess, I think."

Zav added, "She named the spinosaurus Solita."

Humberto rubbed his fingers against his temples. "And she's naming them, so she's bonding with them."

Zo smiled. "It might be hard to believe, but bonds between humans and prehistoric creatures have been documented before. One kid befriended a nundasuchus, I heard about a scientist learning how to ride a pterosaur, and then Seb bonded with the titanoboa, which saved his life—"

"Bad idea." Turning a corner, Ev grunted in disapproval. "Since they're all going to be sent back to their own time, I mean." With food on the mind, he added, "It's like naming your pet cow Steak or Burger. In both of these cases, saying goodbye is inevitable."

Zav groaned as he held his stomach. "Now I want a burger."

Giving Ev a disappointed glare, Zo remarked, "There's nothing wrong with creating attachments to animals, even prehistoric ones. Man's been doing it since the dawn of time."

Ev pulled off the main road to get in the line of cars. "What I'm saying is, do you honestly think dinosaurs will co-exist with us in the present for forever? Our job is *literally* to send them back."

She turned away from him to gaze out the window. "For the time being."

# FORTY-ONE

**GROANING WHILE** sliding out of bed, Earnie wiped the sleep from his eyes. Having dealt with the mini-stroke the day before, he realized he'd slept in longer than expected. As he stood up, the absence of a particular smell confused him. *She's usually made coffee by now.*

Collecting his cellphone from his bedside table, he realized he hadn't plugged it in properly. "Ah shoot, battery's dead." Fiddling with the cord, he got it charging properly and carried on. *You're losing it, Earnie.*

Leaving his bedroom behind, he stepped into the main living space.

No one had been waiting for him.

"Luz?" Her absence troubled him. "Lucero?"

He made it to the fridge, opened the door, and found the pot of leftover stew untouched.

*She didn't come back for food?* He wondered to himself, then thought, *Luz did go through a lot yesterday. Maybe she slept under the stars again, she's done that befo—*

"Mr. Pardy?"

*Knock-knock-knock!*

He veered his gaze to the front door. "Right, right, I'm a-coming."

Evander wore his best smile as Earnie opened the door. "Good morning, Mr. Pardy. Hope you slept well."

"Well enough that I almost didn't wake up," Earnie responded with a chuckle as he waved the group in. "Come on in, everyone. Come on in."

Zoey cleared her throat while entering the house. "I, uh…*apologize* for everything I did and said yester—"

"We're new people today, Miss Zoey." Earnie took her hand in his. "Let's leave yesterday in the past, shall we?"

She made an unexpected grin. "You…remembered my name?"

He smirked. "Can't say you didn't leave an *impression* on me, though."

Zavier walked in and patted Earnie on the back. "Hopefully I won't need a new pair of pants today."

Humberto had been the last to go in. He gazed around at the homey environment of warm colors, pictures of Earnie's family, and a smattering of items which could probably tell a story or two. Then he looked at Earnie, who'd been waiting to welcome him.

"It's been a while, Humberto." Earnie offered his open hand.

Even though Humberto had neglected his kids, he managed a smile and shook hands with the man who'd taken care of Luz on the weekends. "Haven't seen you since you brought her home after *the incident.*"

Ev stood off to the side. "Incident?"

Scratching his head, Earnie worked his semi-groggy brain as he headed for the kitchen. "Eh, Luz biked through one of those rifty things by accident, got chased by some dino…" He started the coffee maker. "…and popped out another rift here on my property."

Zavier made himself comfortable on the couch. "It was back when the rifts were popping up all over the world." Settling in, he tucked a pillow under his arm. "Some say it was a conspiracy, holograms or whatever. We know what really happened."

Ev and Zo gave each other knowing glances.

"And you brought her back home." Humberto stepped over to one of the windows. He spied an animal's head attached to a slender neck poking out from behind the barn. "And now I know why she kept coming back here."

Setting out mugs, Earnie became sheepish. "I told her many times to tell you."

Humberto sighed. "Probably a good thing she didn't, because these animals could have made me a lot of money."

Leaning against the counter, Earnie nodded. "I take it you've cut ties with the cartel?"

Nodding, Humberto stared at the old wooden floorboards. "In the worst way." He lifted his head to gaze out over the property. "Anyway, is Luz okay? We've been trying to call her since last night."

Earnie began pouring coffees for everyone. "She…was

dealing with a lot yesterday." He placed a mug in front of Zoey. "Whenever she's having a bad spell, she'll go out with her critters and sleep under the stars." After pouring another, he handed it to Humberto. "She'll be safe out there, but I've got a walkie if you want it."

"Yes, please," Humberto answered with eagerness.

Finishing the round of drinks, Earnie held onto the coffee pot. "It's in the barn. Make yourselves at home while I go grab it."

Ev picked up a white mug for himself. "Also, thanks for unlocking the gate so we wouldn't have to *trespass* again."

Earnie paused. "Come again?"

Picking up on the old man's unease, Zo reiterated, "The gate. It was open when—"

*Smash!*

The coffee pot hit the floor.

An unstable Earnie had fully woken up. "We *never* unlocked it."

# FORTY-TWO

"LUZ!"

*Ksh-zzt-ksh-zzt.*

"Lucero!"

Sprawled on her back, Luz came to.

An intense throbbing dulled her eyesight. Pins and needles jolted through her right arm, which laid against the boulder she'd hit. "What the—"

*Ksh-zzt-ksh-zzt.*

"Luz, are you there?"

Righting herself to her hands and knees, she realized a creature's body had been casting a shadow onto her, blocking the morning sun. A few blinks helped everything sharpen back to proper vision.

Tess rested a few feet away, having never left her side since the night before. As the young human stirred, she lifted her large head off the ground.

The spinosaurus had taken off after the prehistoric

sparring.

As Luz got to her feet slowly, a dizzy spell sent her forward. She caught herself on the same boulder and squeezed her eyes shut. "Gah, my freaking head."

*Ksh-zzt-ksh-zzt.*

"Lucero, can you hear me?" A voice came through on the walkie. "It's Dad."

Hearing his name and voice made her more awake. "Da... *Dad?*"

Following the haphazard noise of the walkie, she discovered it close to Tess's head. "Hey, girl." Bending down, she propped a hand against the scaley beast. She pressed the side button and spoke. "Dad? Is that really—"

"Oh, *mija!*" He shouted back full of relief. "Luz, haven't you seen Zav's been trying to call you since last night?"

She placed the base of her palm to her forehead. "Uh, last night, I was thrown from...my *horse,* and I—"

"I know about you riding *dinosaurs.*"

Scrunching up her face, she hesitated. "Well, when I flew off the dinosaur, I...must've been knocked right out." She rubbed the back of her head. "Possibly a mild concussion." She staggered back a step. "Most likely."

"You need to get back to the house, but be careful," he emphasized with a graveness in his tone. "The people I used to work for, they're—"

*BLA-KOOOOOOW!*

More attentive than ever, Luz recognized a rifle's blast. "Dad...." The walkie shook in her hand as a nervous lump formed in her throat. "Dad...*s-s-someone's* here."

"Luz!" Humberto shouted through the communication device. "Don't go anywhere near—"

*Ksh-zzt-ksh-zzt.*

Luz turned the volume down as she crouched. Coming around Tess's head, she peeked past to try and find the source of the noise.

A fair bit of distance away, members of El Cazador's cartel had focused on and surrounded the family of minmis.

An armored vehicle lurched forward, blocking one of the dinosaurs from making an escape. One of the men took another shot, sinking a tranquilizer into the neck of a youngling.

Another operative aimed at a defenseless juvenile minmi. "Easy pickings."

The alpha male shrieked as it burst forward, ramming into him and taking out his legs.

In retaliation, two other cartel members fired at it.

One of them laughed. "These dinos don't seem interesting enough to sell."

"Cazador told us to take everything," the other brought up. "And if they don't sell, I'm sure they'll taste good."

Hiding behind the tarbosaurus, Luz couldn't look away, unable to blink. Tears stung her eyes as she observed the cartel poaching the poor dinosaurs.

She'd kept her left hand on the tip of Tess's snout.

Tess groaned, sensing her agitation.

"Luz!" A quieter Humberto called through the walkie. "Luz, are you *safe?*"

Loss and the fear of more of it made Luz freeze in place.

Her relationship with her father had been holding on by a thread.

*BLA-KOOOOOOW!*

Zavier getting kidnapped.

*BLA-KOOOOOOW!*

Her mother.

*BLA-KOOOOOOW!*

The last rifle blast jolted her memories back to a hospital room. The night before Hana had passed, Luz had snuggled up beside her on the bed.

Having taken a deep, shaky breath, she'd whispered: *Mom, I…. I can't imagine not having you around anymore. You'll never see me graduate or achieve things, and if it ever happens, I won't be able to gush over an engagement ring with you, and I can't imagine you not being there to see me walk down the aisle—*

*Oh, hermosa, you need to…be ready,* Hana pleaded, laboring for breath. *As long as…you keep me here*—She'd placed her hand on Luz's chest, right over her heart—*then you will always see me…hear me…feel me. No matter what… you will* never *truly be alone.*

As dizziness dissipated, Luz gazed out over the full picture of the ranch as if true clarity had finally found its place in her mind and heart.

Narrowing her gaze at the cartel, she grit her teeth.

She turned her head to Tess, glanced up to the saddle still attached to her, and patted the dinosaur with justice burning within.

She brought the walkie to her lips. "I need to *save* this ranch."

# FORTY-THREE

**"WHAT IS** she doing?" Humberto stared at the walkie-talkie. "I think she turned it off."

Evander headed for the front door. "She's being stupid… and tactical."

Jittery, Zoey followed her partner outside. "Are you doing what I think you're doing?"

Popping the trunk of his car, Ev didn't hesitate to open a pair of large cases. "I'm getting prepared for anything."

She came to his side. "I'm helping—"

*SKREEEEOOOOOOW!*

One of the austroraptors burst out from behind Earnie's house. It scampered toward them, chirping and screeching.

*BLAM! BLAM!*

A tranquilizer hit it in the thigh.

"Got one, boys!" A burly, balding man laughed, gun in hand as he contacted his associates with an earpiece. "And we've got some *company.*"

Using the trunk door as a shield, Ev finished loading his gun. "Zo, stay back!"

Aramis the austroraptor lost control of its motor functions as the sedative took over. Groaning, it awkwardly stumbled toward the humans.

Zo thrust her arms out, catching the raptor's heavy head. "Jeez, poor thing."

The operative made a mocking cackle. "Aw, look. Someone actually cares about these stupid things."

Putting himself in front of Zo and the austroraptor, Ev aimed at the man. "How about you take your cartel and leave, or die a horrible death in a blaze of gunfire." He unclicked the safety on his weapon. "Your choice."

The man snickered as he started switching to a handgun with real bullets. "El Cazador doesn't care about collateral damage." He took a step toward them. "As long as we get every dinosaur in this—"

*KAOW-KAAAAOOOOW!*

Porthos bolted into view and approached from the left.

*R-R-R-R-SKREEEEAAAAOOOOW!*

Athos snarled, darting in from the right.

They immediately identified their incapacitated brethren.

The man cursed, holding an open hand out to one of the austroraptors while keeping his gun on the other. "Stay... Stay back!"

Both dinosaurs vocalized to each other, forming a plan of attack as they slowly converged.

With the guy's attention off of them, Ev placed his finger on the trigger. "And *adiós* to—"

"*Wait!*" Zo whispered, identifying cues from the raptors. "*He's* the threat. If you shoot, they'll think we are, too."

As the man's legs locked in place, he shot a warning shot into the sky while keeping his free hand up. "Back up, you stupid lizards! *Back it up!*"

A few feet away, Athos opened his mouth wide and hissed.

As soon as the operative focused on it, Porthos leapt forward. Pounding the man into the ground, the force of the strike also knocked the gun away.

Aramis bolted to join in the takedown.

Their claws dug into the screaming man as they nipped at his body with their elongated, toothy jaws.

Zoey nodded to herself. "*Austro la vista,* baby."

"Leave the raptor and take this," Ev instructed while prepping a specialized weapon. Unlike normal bullets, the ammo glowed as he loaded it in and handed it over. "This is a two-part process. Fire the transponder clip onto a creature, and when it attaches, press the button on the side of the gun." He glanced around every few seconds as he pulled his phone out. "Gotta text Seb to let him know what's happening."

After lowering Aramis the austroraptor gently to the gravel, Zo received the non-lethal artillery. "Does this do what I think it does?"

Ev grinned. "Try it out on this raptor, it's already tranq'd."

"Really?" She studied it for a couple seconds before shooting Aramis with a clip. "And then I press *this* to—"

*ZEEUU-BWOOOOM!*

A concentrated beam of bright blueish light whisked the austroraptor away.

The momentary flash caught the attention of Porthos and Athos for a split second before they resumed their onslaught.

Zo stared in absolute shock and awe. "When did SauraCorps get *teleporter* guns?"

"Seb said he met with some spy guy, a gadget *specialist* or something." Ev finished arming himself and shut the trunk. "It teleports dinos to a special facility back at HQ."

She couldn't contain her fascination. "Heck yeah it does!"

With a bloody arm outstretched, the cartel member cried out, "Hel… Help, *por fav*—"

*SKREEAAOOW!*

*Snap-Crunch!*

Porthos and Athos finished off their enemy.

Ev and Zo pulled their grimacing gazes away and headed back up the front porch. Getting inside, they found everyone else glued to the windows, observing the dinosaur attack.

Earnie snickered. "All for one, and one for all."

Coming right over to the homeowner, Zo placed a hand on his shoulder. "Just wondering, you wouldn't happen to have any more dinosaurs trained for riding, would you?"

He raised both eyebrows. "Well, last I saw, Tess the 'tarbo' is with Luz." He paused, unsure about his other prehistoric steed. "Tango is Tess's brother, but he's a bit more…unruly, and hasn't quite been broken yet."

She smirked. "Sounds perfect."

Evander checked the other side of the house while

overhearing the conversation. "Uh, you sure about that, Zo?"

Holstering the gun in her pants, Zoey redid her hair into a ponytail. "This is gonna be *epic*."

# FORTY-FOUR

**"FORGET MIGUEL,"** Blanca ordered. "He's gone."

The team had just overheard their associate's fate over their comms.

Needing to keep her crew on track, Blanca reminded them, "Transports will be here soon." Blanca sat in the safety of the armored vehicle. "Speed it up! The more we take, the more we'll make."

A pair of cartel members finished tying up the last minmi. "What's the next catch?"

Blanca shrugged. "Whatever we come across is ours for the taking."

Her right hand clung to the top of the steering wheel. She adjusted her side mirror, checking the area behind them for any creatures.

"You guys...*feel* that?" one of her squad remarked.

Another clipped a new mag of tranquilizers and pressed his hand into the ground. He detected the slight tremor.

"It's not an earthquake."

Awkwardly hoisting herself up and partially through the window to look over the vehicle's roof, Blanca scanned all she could see.

A cloud of dirt and dust masked the source.

"Is that...." Blanca shimmied back inside. "Dammit—everyone, *get moving!*"

"What's going on over—"

"*Stampede!*"

Honks, bellows, and shrieks intermingled with thundering stomps.

"Take cover!"

Scrambling into their vehicles, some of the cartel barely made it.

Peggy the parasaurolophus and the rest of her species barrelled through. One of them bodychecked an armored SUV as another trampled a man.

Among the variety of dinosaurs in the herd, a styracosaurus charged at Blanca's SUV.

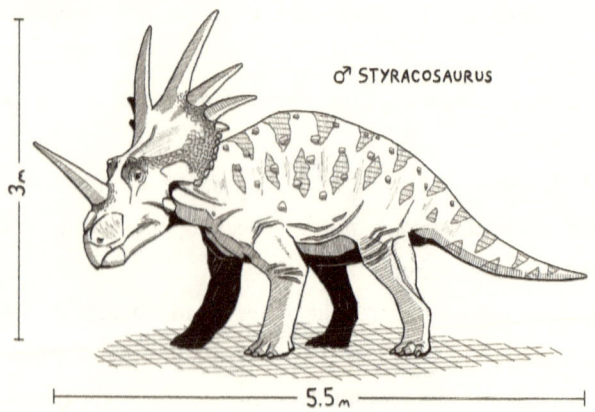

♂ STYRACOSAURUS

3ᴍ

5.5ᴍ

"Oh, frig–" She slammed her good foot on the gas, spinning the tires until they finally made traction.

*SMASH!*

The armored vehicle's rear took the brunt of the impact.

With the wheels still intact, Blanca shot forward and out of the way. She turned her gaze away from the herd, sucked in an alarmed breath, and hammered the brake. "*Jesuchris*—"

*RRRROOOOOOUUUUUUHHRR!*

Tess the tarbosaurus sprinted directly at her.

Lucero rode atop the dinosaur with determination in her eyes.

Readjusting into reverse, a frantic Blanca wrenched the steering wheel to the right.

Roaring once again, Tess drove her left foot into Blanca's hood. One of her large claws broke through the windshield, driving shards of glass inward.

One of El Cazador's men hung outside of his own passenger window and shot at some of the creatures. Some darts missed, while others made direct hits.

Tess withdrew her scaley foot from the vehicle, allowing her rider to look down and into the front seat.

"I'd suggest you leave this ranch now," Luz called down with conviction. "Before we turn your cartel into a trampled mess."

Blanca reached for her rifle. "You have no idea what you're—"

*RRRROOOOOOUUUUUUHHRR!*

Luz had given Tess a hand-pat signal to cut Blanca off.

"Sorry, did you say you're leaving?"

Pointing the barrel through the hole in the windshield, Blanca gritted her teeth. "Guess again, *chica.*"

*BLAM!*

The dart soared through the air.

*Thip!*

It made contact with Tess's neck.

"No!" Luz clicked her tongue, urging her prehistoric steed to advance. While on the move, she left the saddle and clung to the straps connected to the bridle.

Tess swayed her head side to side as the tranquilizer began taking effect.

Grazing the dart with her fingertips, Luz stretched herself out once more.

Satisfied with her precision, Blanca aimed again. "Love hunting big game."

*SMASH!*

*BLAM!*

Getting spun around, Blanca missed and lost her rifle as she got knocked around within the damaged vehicle. After a couple of uncontrollable turns, she faced who'd thwarted her.

Another tarbosaurus lowered its head to peer inside.

Backing up, it stomped its heavy foot into the ground and snarled.

"Tango, mind your manners, now." Zoey pretended to scold the dinosaur, then got jerked forward. "Whoa, boy!" She snapped and yanked the reins back for control, then glared down at her enemy. "And how's Gimpy Cazador's knee today? If you stick around long enough, I'm sure my friend would love to take out your other one."

"Think you have us beat?" Blanca yelled up and laughed. "Think again."

More armored vehicles and outfitted transport trucks advanced onto the property.

*WHOP-WHOP-WHOP-WHOP-WHOP!*

After pulling the dart out of a groggy Tess's neck, Luz gazed upward.

Off in the distance, a pair of military-style helicopters entered the ranch's airspace.

"*Dios mío.*" Luz climbed back over and into the saddle. "Tess, this doesn't look good."

# FORTY-FIVE

**"LOOKS LIKE** some kind of transport is about to pull in." Evander opened one of the windows and pointed his gun through it. He'd decided to stay behind and deem Earnie's home their base of operations and the last line of defense. "Cazador's organization is no joke."

Earnie came up beside him. "Anything me and ol' Roxie can do to help?"

Giving a grunt of respect, Ev frowned. "I'd feel better if you didn't get involved in the violence, Mr. Pardy." He likened Earnie's willingness to that of his fallen military friends. "Clearly, you're the heart and soul of this place."

"Which is exactly why everything on this ranch is depending on me," Earnie rebutted, staring out at the oversized transport trucks. He'd never witnessed so many people trespassing onto his property before. "If Marilyn were alive to see this, she'd be right by my side."

Ev chuckled at the image in his mind. "Was she a feisty

one?"

"Heck, she'd already be out there hollering, cussing, and firing a few rounds at 'em."

"Sounds like she was quite the woman."

Earnie grinned. "*Quite's* an understatement."

"What about us?" Humberto stood by the dining room table, keeping an eye out along the back of the ranch house. "Are there any other weapons we—" He glanced at his son crouching in the living area, whom he'd almost lost the day before. "—I mean, *I* can use?"

Out front, another SUV pulled up.

Ev and Earnie ducked and peeked just over the windowsill.

Four cartel members exited the vehicle. One of them spotted their fallen colleague and immediately pulled out a handgun.

*SKREEEEOOOOOOW!*

Porthos leapt from the house's roof to the SUV's roof, and bit down onto the man's shoulder. Flinging him off to the side, it slid down the windshield and vaulted onto another.

Ev took advantage of their attention on the solo austroraptor.

*BLAM! BLAM!*

Earnie pulled Roxie's trigger.

*BLA-KOOOOOOW!*

All four of El Cazador's men had been neutralized.

Ev and Earnie glanced at each other and fist-bumped.

"That's one wave down...with more to come," Ev mentioned with unease. "If we make it out of this alive, I suggest you put up a 'Beware of Dog' sign by your gate."

Earnie smirked. "Only when threatened. They're actually sweet critters once you get to know them."

Creeping up behind the long-necked shunosaurus, two of El Cazador's men parked their truck and left the doors open. Nearly a hundred feet away from it, they prepped their weapons.

"If this one turns on us, gonna have to watch its clubbed tail, Perez."

"Let me have this one." The other man set up and rested his rifle on a boulder. "How many cc's do you think this one will take, Sosa?"

"Do three just to be sa—"

*Mmraaaaaah.*

Both cartel members glanced at each other in utter confusion.

Behind them, a massive mound of thick hair repositioned and stood on all fours.

"The heck is *that?*" Whipping out a gun, Sosa held off on shooting it.

*Mmraaaaaaaahh.*

Monty the shaggy megatherium groaned and blinked a few times at them. He didn't know what to make of the two new humans.

Rolling over to reposition and point his weapon at it, Perez asked, "Boss said to secure *everything*, right?"

Sosa nodded. "Whatever we find out here."

After a shrug, Perez aimed at the giant ground sloth's shoulder.

*BLAM!*

Monty's super-thick fur stopped the tranq dart from sticking, and it dropped to the ground. He glanced at the impact spot, then back at the intruders.

*MMRAAAAAAAAAAAAAAAH!*

Another two shots couldn't penetrate Monty's pelt.

"Get back in the truck!" Sosa yelled to Perez as they both embarked the vehicle and slammed the doors shut, and didn't bother with seatbelts.

Sosa turned the key and pressed on the gas.

*WHUMP-CLANG!*

They couldn't move.

Perez turned in his seat. "Come on, *go go go!*"

Monty had seized the truck's tailgate with his foot-long claws. Lifting the backend off the dirt and grass, he wailed once more before engaging more muscles.

"What are you waiting for?" Perez shouted at Sosa before hanging himself out the window. "Let me try one more ti-*whooooaaaa!*"

*CRUNCH-SMASH!*

Upside down, both men got jostled and knocked unconscious within the truck's cab.

Snorting, Monty growled one last time as he turned away. Scratching his behind as he left the humans, he plucked a gooseberry bush from the ground and munched away.

"You guys realize we're done, right?" Humberto spoke out loud, still keeping an eye on the windows closest to him. "El Cazador has an army. There's no way out of this." He glanced at his son, afraid of losing both of his children for good. "*We're done.*"

Ev recalled losing his squad. He'd done everything he could back then. Now, they needed some kind of hope. "Listen, I know this seems dire, and I can't guarantee all of us will make it…" He glanced around at the other three as he delivered his little speech. "…but Zoey and I will do everything in our power and ability to keep everyone as safe as possible."

Zavier spotted a couple of figures slinking past the kitchen window. "Uh, guys, I think—"

*WHAM!*

The back door burst open.

Six of El Cazador's men stormed in.

Humberto tried to fight one off. "Torrez, you don't have to do thi—"

*THWACK!*

Another struck him in the back with the butt of their rifle.

They tossed him toward Zavier, congregated around the Sanchez men, and pointed their weapons at them.

Ev lowered his weapon, careful to avoid any collateral damage.

Startled by the intrusion, Earnie stagger-spun around and pointed his firearm at the group. "Hey, leave them alo—"

"Drop your weapons, *amigos.*" El Cazador stepped in

and stood right in front of the doorway. With a threatening stare, he made eye contact with every single opposer in the open room. "Let's have ourselves a little discussion."

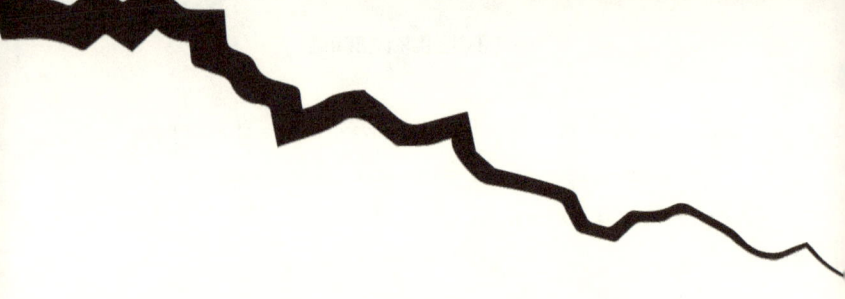

# FORTY-SIX

***WHOP-WHOP-WHOP-WHOP-WHOP!***

Chopping of the helicopter blades freaked out most of the dinosaurs, causing them to scatter.

In the aftermath of the stampede, a couple of vehicles had been damaged. As well, a number of operatives had either been injured or trampled.

Still alive and protected, Blanca gazed around at her decimated crew.

Backing away from the ravaged cartel, Lucero guided Tess over to the familiar woman. "Should we retreat?" She picked up on the dinosaur's groan and gave her a scratch. "Not sure how much longer Tess can go for."

"She'll burn it off quickly," Zoey told her while struggling for control of Tango. "It'll take more than…one tranq to take her down."

The two dinosaurs greeted each other.

Tango whined as he nudged his sister in the neck.

"But will *we* be okay?" Luz stared back at the incoming helicopters. "I don't... I don't see a way out of this."

Squinting as random ideas popped in her head, Zo grabbed her phone and clicked on a contact. "Hey, Seb, cool new tele-guns, by the way. Where exactly does it send the targets?"

Sebastian paused. "In this case, every clip is calibrated for specific enclosures. Why?"

"Can you reprogram the next few for me?"

"Again, *why?*"

"Because the ranch is under attack..." She put on a Schwarzenegger impression. "...and El Cazador has choppas."

Revving the engine of her partially-destroyed yet driveable vehicle, Blanca called out, "Might as well give yourselves up now. We can cover more territory with our birds in the sky."

Luz's eyes flared open. "*Territory.*"

Zo finished up her call. "Yes, reposition to there, pretty please." Then she turned to the teen. "What are you—"

"We need to move, now!" Getting Tess to obey, Luz waved Zo onward.

As the tarbosaurus duo carried on, Blanca fished around the floor of her vehicle for her phone. "Come on, *come on.*" Her fingertips brushed against it before nudging it toward her. Picking it back up, she made a call. "Cruz, come in, Cruz!"

"*Sí*, Blanca, sorry we're late."

Blinded by rage, she shifted into four-wheel-drive. "Radio Ulises and go after the two riding the...whatever dinos those are!"

Galloping side by side, Tess and Tango allowed their

riders to converse.

Zoey yelled over the thunderous sprinting, "Where are you taking us?"

Luz pointed. "There's a lake up ahead."

Zo smirked. "If there is, we'll all be dead."

The teen squinted at her. "Did you just reference *Princess Bride?*"

"That a bad thing?"

"It was my mom and I's all-time favorite movie." Luz grinned, then focused on the body of water up ahead. "Split off and ride along the opposite side from me."

Still unsure of the plan, Zo trusted her.

*WHOP-WHOP-WHOP-WHOP!*

Both helicopters gained on them.

Taking off to the right, Zo unhooked her shoes from the stirrups and maneuvered into riding reverse. Tele-gun in hand, she aimed at one of the choppers. Letting her arms sway in tandem with Tango's sprint, she found the rhythm.

*BLAM-BLAM!*

The first shot missed.

As for the second, it attached itself to the hull.

Zo wore a mischievous smile. "Ice, ice, baby."

She pressed the button on the side of the gun.

*ZEEEEUUUU-BWOOOOM!*

A crackling beam of space-time energy captured the helicopter, whisking it away from the ranch.

"*¡Hijole!*" Cruz shouted, baffled by the sudden disappearance of his cohorts. "What the heck just happened to Ulises and his squad? They're…*gone!*"

"Stay on them," Blanca demanded through speakerphone. "Maybe keep some kind of distance."

Keeping both targets in sight, Cruz flew directly to the middle of the lake. Hovering over the water, he lowered the aircraft as his squad readied their weapons.

The spinning blades created large ripples in the water below.

Noticing movement inside of the helicopter, Zo gripped the reins. *Hope Luz knows what she's doing.*

On the opposite side, Luz shielded her eyes from the sunlight as she gazed out over the lake. *Don't fail me now.*

One of the shooters locked onto Luz and Tess.

The man behind him took aim at Zo and Tango.

His bottom peripheral picked up on a swimming mass beneath them.

A scaley sail's crest protruded from the lake's surface.

Turning his gaze down, he screamed out, "Go up *now!* Climb, *climb!*"

Cruz called back, "What are you—"

*KER-SPLASH!*

*RAAAAAA-HI-I-I-I-I-I-I-I-ISSSS!*

Solita the spinosaurus had propelled herself upward.

Clasping her right hand's three claws onto a bottom rung of the aircraft, she weighed it down as they attempted to ascend. Slamming her left forelimb closer to the cockpit, one of her claws shattered the glass, slashing into Cruz's lower body.

Losing balance and control, the helicopter turned sideways. As the blades chopped into the murky water, they lost propulsion and failed.

Climbing out and onto the side of the aircraft still above the surface, the two armed men coughed out water while regaining control of their rifles.

Backs to each other, the frantic pair muttered expletives and glanced all around.

"Do we give it everything we've got?"

"Might as we—*aaaaaauuuugh!*"

Jaws had exploded toward them, snagging one and pulling him under.

On his own, the last cartel member trembled in stance and breath.

Red had begun mixing into the water.

*BLAM-BLAM-BLAM-BLAM-BLAM!*

He roared while unloading his rounds into the lake.

Nothing.

Eerie silence drifted around him.

"Come on, you frigging dino—"

*HI-I-I-I-I-I-I-I-I-ISSSS!*

Solita clambered onto the helicopter and knocked him into the lake.

With her sleek and powerful body glistening in the sunlight, she snarled before diving back in with her mouth open wide.

Slowing to a stop at the lake's edge, Blanca couldn't believe what had just transpired. Attempting to make contact with Ulises, every effort failed. "No, no no no, *no!*"

## FIVE MINUTES EARLIER

*ZEEEEUUUU-BWOOOOM!*

Temperatures dropped drastically.

A tumultuous snowstorm whipped its contents through the open doors and into the helicopter.

As everyone else panicked, Ulises, barely able to control his direction, threw his arm up over his eyes.

*CRUNCH-SMASH!*

Colliding into the side of a hefty iceberg, El Cazador's men jostled and tumbled within the helicopter.

Incessant alerts filled the aircraft as it plunged into the icy Antarctic waters below.

## PRESENT DAY

"Freaking right, Solita!" Lucero cheered while atop Tess. "That was epic…and intense."

"Get off the dinosaur." Blanca called up from her armored vehicle while pointing her gun at the girl. "*Now.*"

Hands up, Luz held the reins in one hand. "Still think you can win this?"

Having left Tango behind to make a quieter approach, Zoey hid among some brush.

"This isn't about winning or losing, little girl," Blanca retorted while unclipping her seatbelt. "It's about *surviving.*" Leaving the protection of the damaged vehicle, she fought to stand on her injured leg. "Now get off that damn dinosaur, or else you'll lose everyone and everything you've ever love—"

"Go ahead," Luz yelled back. "Just do it already."

Blanca hesitated.

Still hiding, Zo peeked over some bushes, perplexed by the teen's plea.

"I've already lost." Luz carried on, dropping her hands to her lap. "My mom...she *was* everything." Adrenaline dropped within her, and she gave in to the emotional low. "She would've loved this ranch, and the more I spend time here, the more I see *so much of her* in it. Its diverse beauty, the soothing tranquility..." She sniffled and made a single chuckle. "...its ferocity when threatened."

Blanca's lower lip twitched. "Get down from—"

"All this time, I didn't want to face her loss. But all I've really been avoiding and fighting is a new perspective." Luz locked eyes with her. "Now I know...what *true love* really is."

As Blanca's hands trembled, she eventually gave in and lowered her gun. Hearing someone so young say something so sincere and profound made her realize what she truly needed, but lacked.

Sneaking forward, Zo disarmed and forced zip-ties onto her in swift fashion. After collecting the gun for herself, Zo pushed Blanca into the vehicle's side. "If I were you, I'd warn the rest of your cartel buddies to—"

*Buzzzz. Buzzzz.*

Blanca's phone vibrated within her jacket.

Taking it out, Zo allowed the call and enabled the

speakerphone.

El Cazador's voice came through. "Blanca, do you have Lucero and the other woman?"

Prodding the loaded handgun into her captive's ribcage, Zo whispered, "Say yes."

Disgust on her face, Blanca scoffed. "Really? Can't you see how many of us there are out there on this *pathetic* little ranch ready to take everything it has? You have no play here—"

*ZEEEEUUUU-BWOOOOM!*

*BWOOOOM! BWOOOOM! BWOOOOM! BWOOOOM!*

SauraCorps tactical personnel teleported throughout the ranch, surrounding and taking out cartel members with military-style precision and ability.

The impressive show of support made Luz's eyes well up.

Even Zo breathed a sigh of true relief. "You were saying?"

A reluctant Blanca finally answered her father, "*Sí.*"

"Bring them back to the house," El Cazador instructed. "I need some…*insurance.*"

# FORTY-SEVEN

**"NOW, I** hate repeating myself 'cause it's a waste of my precious time left on this planet," Earnie growled at the cartel kingpin. "Threaten me all you want, but this is my home, and no offer you make will ever be good enough."

El Cazador sat across from him at the dining room table. "Mr. Pardy, like I said, I'm sure we can come to some agreement without needless killing."

"What did I just say about threats?" Earnie snorted, holding his own. "Because that still sounds like one."

Evander, Humberto, and Zavier all sat in the living room portion of the open space.

The half-dozen of El Cazador's men surrounded them.

"Dad," Zav gave him a solemn stare. "If we don't make it—"

"*Mijo.*" Humberto leaned toward him, making their foreheads touch. "I love you, more than you'll ever know."

Relaxed, El Cazador propped his feet up on one of the

chairs and grinned. "Mr. Pardy, you really don't see it do you? Even a fraction of the money we could make from all the creatures here would definitely give you a comfortable life."

"My life's already comfy as is," Earnie countered, crossing his arms at the uninvited guest. "What more do I need?"

Shrugging, El Cazador leaned his head to the side. "Protection, perhaps?"

"From you dimwits, *perhaps.*"

*SLAM!*

El Cazador struck the table with an open palm. "You don't like your time being wasted, and I don't like playing games."

Silent, Earnie glanced over at the small group of new friends. He nibbled on his bottom lip as he took each of their lives into consideration. Stalling could only go on for so long, but he hoped it would buy them enough time for someone to save them.

Noticing the old man's glances, El Cazador relieved the wooden chair of his feet and stood up. "If you need convincing…" He drew his hunting knife from behind his back. "…then perhaps I'll start calling myself *El Carnicero.*"

Ev didn't like the tone used along with the word. "What's that?"

Tensing up, Zavier translated, "*Butcher.*"

Nearing the barn, Zoey slowed the armored vehicle to a stop.

Lucero hopped out of the front passenger seat and bolted toward Earnie's house. Making it to the corner of the hefty building, she halted.

Men she didn't recognize had made their way inside her second home.

Staying in the vehicle, Zo kept an eye on Blanca sitting in the backseat. "What's the matter, Luz?"

Backtracking over, Luz placed her hands on the window's bottom edge. "I think the cartel is—"

"My father would be in there," Blanca remarked, annoyed with her uncomfortable wrist restraints and the cumbersome leg cast. "He's probably killed your friends and family by now, or is in the process of it."

Zo placed a hand on one of Luz's. "And there's a chance they're still alive."

Chewing on the inside of her cheek, Luz shook her head in defeat. "What are we supposed to do now? They all have guns and—"

"Luz, listen to me, okay?" Zo took the teen's hands fully in hers. "I'm willing to do whatever it takes. Now tell me, is there anything I need to know about this area? Any dinos or anything we can use to our advantage?"

Luz squeezed Zo's hands tighter. "A few things…I guess."

"Good." Zo angled herself to look back at their captive. "Last question, how much of a daddy's girl are you?"

"My dire wolves are always hungry." El Cazador pointed the

knife's tip at Zavier. "I'm sure they would *enjoy* their meat young and tender…" He swung it over to Evander, who reacted with a wary grunt. "…and they get so animated when tearing into firm muscle…" Then he brought the blade up to Humberto's throat. "…but I'm sure they would *love* even more meat on the bones."

Closing his eyes, Humberto whimpered.

Bringing his face closer to him, El Cazador grabbed the back of Humberto's hair. "Especially when it's the meat of a *traitor.*"

"*El Cazadoooor!*"

Everyone's attention focused on the voice from outside.

"Who was that?" The summoned cartel leader peered out the back windows. Unable to locate the source, he sneered. "Octavio, go find out who it is."

Making it to the back door, Octavio paused at the threshold. "But, Jefe, there are still raptors out there."

Giving him a piercing glare, El Cazador added a wrathful grin. "Either the raptors kill you, or I'll kill you for disobeying my orders."

Gulping down a nervous lump, Octavio said a silent prayer before stepping outside.

Rifle up, he swung it back and forth.

Sweat dripped from his brow thanks to the hot Texas sun, and the knowledge that raptors could strike from any location.

Since the back door had been left open, El Cazador strolled over and called out, "Do you see anyone?"

Octavio shouted over his shoulder, "Nothing ye—"

*BLAM! BLAM!*

*ZEEEEUUUU-BWOOOOM!*

Teleported away, only Octavio's footprints were left in the dirt.

Witnessing their colleague vanishing into thin air, the remaining cartel members became frantic and muttered among themselves in Spanish.

Even El Cazador flared his eyelids open, more aware of his enemy's abilities. Once an unnerving silence settled in, he called out, "Show yourselves!"

Concealed by the opposite side of the barn, Zoey yelled back, "How about we hash this out on the far side of this barn?"

El Cazador chuckled. "And why would I do—"

Thrust past the corner of the barn, a restrained and gagged Blanca staggered and winced.

She locked eyes with her father.

Zoey pulled Blanca back behind the structure. "Bring everyone out."

Tearing his stare away, El Cazador glanced around at his men and their detainees. "Let's go, as they said. *Vamos!*"

Prodding Evander, Humberto, Zavier, and Earnie ahead of them, El Cazador and his crew kept their heads on swivels.

"Do you think it's Luz?" Zavier whispered to his dad.

Humberto sighed. "If it is, I hope she's okay."

Coming around the corner, they found Zoey, Luz, and a restrained Blanca waiting for them at the far end.

With hostages on either side, a new kind of tension took

hold of everyone.

"Stay right there," Zo demanded, keeping Blanca in front of her and Luz behind.

Snickering, El Cazador cracked his neck. "Is this your first time, *señorita?*"

"Can't say I've taken down a cartel before," Zo countered. "Might celebrate with nachos afterward. Any good recs, *El Basura?*"

"Did she just call me...*trash?*" El Cazador laughed. "She's spicy, this one."

Ev snorted. "You have no idea."

"Now, at the same time..." Zo continued with her negotiations. "...we'll let our respective hostages switch— "

"Do you really think you have the upper hand here?" El Cazador began pacing. "Because to me, really, you have *no play.*"

An internal shock struck Blanca in her core.

He waved an open hand to his human bargaining chips. "Four to one is better odds for me to get everything I want, no?" Stepping closer to them, he nodded to one of his men.

*Thwack!*

Humberto had been shoved forward and to the ground.

"No!" Luz screamed, getting held back by Zo. "No... *Dad,* no."

Raising his voice, Humberto expected the next few moments to be his last. "Lucero, Zavier, close your eyes, please."

Laughing, El Cazador mocked the display of sincere fatherly love. "Aw, so sweet seeing a *real* family bond."

Still gagged, Blanca gawked at her father.

He noticed her taking offense. "Blanca, Blanca, *Blanca*. Did you really think I had so much money that I wouldn't notice you *stealing* more than your fair share from me? You disappoint me, *girl*." Knife still in his grasp, El Cazador came behind Humberto. "And this traitor here...he isn't even worth the trade."

Evander tensed and braced himself. Pressing his thumb against the base of his other, he worked hypotheticals out in his mind. Trying to take on all of the men behind him would require maximum effort. The Sanchez men and Earnie were still variables he couldn't afford to lose.

His gaze met Zoey's.

She offered a subtle nod.

He responded with a grimace.

Luz stared at her dad with tears in her eyes. *This can't be real.* Her head throbbed as everything threatened to collapse with one simple act.

*Whump!*

"Oh...G-*aaaah*-God." Earnie had slumped to the ground, shuddering as his shaky hands held his chest. "My... My-my *heart*—s-s-s-*stroke*."

All eyes fixated on him.

"Earnie!" Luz cried out. "His strokes are getting worse."

Even El Cazador turned away from Humberto and scowled. "Is...he really—"

*Whack!*

Evander spun as he freed his hands from their restraints, bodychecking one of the cartel members. As another pointed their rifle, he crouched, drove a jab into their right knee, and flipped him over his shoulder while relieving them of their rifle.

Two bullets later, only four of El Cazador's guards remained.

Humberto took the opportunity to get up and flee toward his daughter. "Come on, Zav!"

Another operative turned to fire at Evander.

Zavier collided into the man with a war cry. As they both tumbled, Zav couldn't regain his footing to get back up and run.

The cartel member struck the teen's gut with the butt of his weapon before repositioning it to shoot.

From behind, Evander slung the strap of his newly acquired rifle around their neck, pulling them backward and down into the hard ground.

Zoey shoved Blanca away and aimed her tele-gun at another guard.

*BLAM!*

*ZEEEEUUUU-BWOOOOM!*

As the space-time energy beam dissipated, Ev's fist connected with the last man's head.

Furious at how fast his team had fallen apart, El Cazador hollered, "None of you will leave this ranch alive!" Crazed, he backed away from Evander and the group of ex-hostages. "This ranch… *will…be…mine!*"

On both sides of Zoey and Luz, Athos and Porthos appeared.

Thundering footsteps intensified as Tess and Tango came into sight before slowing to stand behind Ev, Zavier, and a motionless Earnie.

Trapped in the middle, El Cazador glanced back and forth.

A different vibration made its way through his feet and legs.

"The heck is going on now?" Ev checked the surroundings.

Sitting up, Earnie dusted himself off. "Must be another rift, or—"

"Whoa!" Zav flinched and stepped back. "I thought you were *dead*, man!"

Ev grunt-chuckled. "Thanks for the distraction, Earnie."

Slight wind picked up around El Cazador as he picked up on a whiff of static.

*CRRRRACK-ACK-ACK! ZAP! CRACKLE! SNAP!*

Less than five feet away from him, a time rift materialized.

Captured by its ethereal beauty, he gasped.

Beside the barn, the anomalous window displayed a primeval world. Grassland teemed with prehistoric creatures, and various pterosaurs soared through the ancient sky.

"*Dios mío.*" El Cazador let his mouth hang open, taking it all in. "It's beautiful."

Tango and Tess sniffed the air as a familiar scent reached their nostrils.

On the prehistoric side, an older tarbosaurus came into view.

*RRRROOOOOOUUUUUUHR!*

Both tarbosaurus adolescents took hesitant steps toward the time they'd once lived in. Getting even closer, they groaned in excitement.

Their mother poked her head through.

*ROOH-UUHR! ROOH-UUHR!*

Dodging their steps and rushing closer to the barn, El Cazador stood in awe.

"*Padre?*"

Taken out of his trance, he turned his head to find Blanca limping her way over to him. "Oh, *mija,* come here. Let me help with this." Cutting her zip-ties off, he allowed her to lean on him. "We'll be talking about your embezzlement when we get out of—"

"*Jefe,*" she replied while gazing downward. "I never wanted this."

He wore a fake grin. "Don't worry, I'm sure we can work somethi—"

"I quit."

*Thwack!*

Blanca punched him in the throat. "Even dinosaurs care for their young better than you ever cared for me."

Choking, he dropped his hunting knife. "Blanc… Blanca, I—"

"All your money *blinded* you from the only thing I ever needed from you." Summoning all her strength, she engaged her leg muscles. "This…is…*enough.*"

Even with the clunky leg brace on, she ran at her father, seized him, and headed straight for the rift's coursing and crackling electrical frame.

As they both entered its supercharged space-time energy, Blanca roared as El Cazador yelled out her name one last time.

# FORTY-EIGHT

**RELIEF SWELLED** over everyone.

Earnie had made it over to the barn. "Come on inside, everyone. Come on, now."

Having their own little moment, Humberto and Lucero hugged each other harder than ever before. Zavier soon joined in on the love.

Considering the last two days' events, a collective family embrace had been more than needed.

Smiling, Evander held out his hand to Zoey. "How'd it go out there, Beaumont?"

She gave him an odd stare and pointed at his hand. "What's that for?"

"What do you mea—"

Cutting him off with a hug, she tightened her grip. "Happy to see you're still alive, sugar bear."

Rolling his eyes while still in her arms, he smirked. "You, too…*Gorgeous.*"

"Look who's finally playing along." She pulled away and patted him on the arm. "Also, how'd you free yourself?"

Zav piped up. "I was wondering the same thing."

Ev shrugged. "Dislocated my thumb."

"Oh, dang." Zav rubbed his hands together. "Can you teach me that, in case I ever get kidnapped again?"

Humberto shook his head. "Let's not mention that again, shall we?"

Leaving her father, Luz marched straight over to Earnie. "Don't *ever* fake having a stroke on me again."

He let out a sheepish chuckle. "It worked, didn't it? And don't worry, I ain't ready to become worm food just yet."

Giving each other a hug, they even shed a couple of tears.

"Love you lots, Earnie."

"Aw, love you right back, Luz."

"Pretty sure some paramedics are around here who can take a look at Earnie," Zo mentioned, pulling out her phone. "Seb called in the whole SauraCorps cavalry. They all teleported here like Thor's *Infinity War* arrival. Should've seen it, it was epic."

Having made their way over to the open barn door, Ev and Zo observed the still active time rift and the family of reconnecting tarbosauruses.

"First time seeing a rift?" Ev simply asked.

"Yep." After sending a text, she took a picture of the rift with her phone. "Other than the whole 'Beam me up, Sebby' thing, this is new for me."

"How'd the new gun work out for you?"

"Sent a helicopter to Antarctica, and those other two

guys." She spoke all casual. "Oh, but a spinosaurus *demolished* the other chopper. Hold on, I took a video."

"Actually...." Ev uncrossed his arms and rushed back toward the house to reclaim his cellphone. "Need to call Sebastian, he should really be here."

"This place is *incredible,*" Sebastian remarked, standing on the back deck of Earnie's home. "That's a shunosaurus over there, isn't it? And did I see austroraptors run by?"

Lucero grinned. "You know your dinosaurs."

"I'd hope so." He laughed. "They're *literally* my business."

Zavier carried a tray of iced tea out to the group. "Did you...have anything to do with that massive rift that spanned a block of San Francisco two years ago?"

Sebastian winced. "How much will it take for you to never mention that again?"

Evander grabbed two drinks and handed one off to Zoey. "Speaking of *business,* it's about time we get down to it."

Taking a sip of his own, Earnie sat forward in his deck chair as a pair of SauraCorps paramedics finished up tending to him. "I'm hoping your offer is better than El Cazador's."

Watching the glyptodons mosey over, Sebastian smiled. "Well, there are new variables that come to mind." He turned to look at Earnie and Luz. "I have to say, the fact you two have been able to run this place so well without people finding out until now is quite the feat."

Humberto chuckled, which caught his daughter's attention. "I'd have to agree."

"And that rift over there…" Sebastian added, then took a thoughtful sip of iced tea. Unable to see it from Earnie's deck, he could still hear the crackle of space-time energy. "…normally they close by now, but this one is staying *open* for some reason. I'd have to get our scientists down here, but…what happened before it opened in the first place?"

Earnie brought up, "Those rifts have been opening off and on since about two years ago."

Placing her glass on a small table, Zo stood up to spend time with the glyptodons. "I shot one of the cartel guys with the tele-gun. Could the energy hitting the ground… with the gallax—whatever you called it—embedded in the earth be what triggered it?"

"That's possible." Sebastian leaned against the railing. "Won't know until—"

*Z-Z-ZAP! ZZZZEEEEUUUU-POP!*

Everyone perked up at the noise of the rift closing.

Zav pointed in its general direction. "Was that it?"

"It must've just closed," Luz answered, curious if Tess and Tango had returned to prehistoric time with their mother. "I'm too exhausted to go check."

"Hmm." Sebastian tapped his fingers against the glass. "Well, I guess…it could still work."

Ev finished his drink. "I like to hurt vague people."

Earnie snorted. "You've got issues, young man."

Nodding to himself, Sebastian went over and sat down beside the ranch owner. "How would you like to work for

SauraCorps?" Then he turned to address Luz. "We could also use some interns, if you're up for it."

"Sorry, Mr. Sharpe, but…" Earnie scratched his forehead. "…I'm not sure I follow."

"If that rift and possibly more keep popping up on your property, then there's always the chance of creatures making a home here. So, why not make this ranch another base of operations for SauraCorps?" Sebastian explained, growing more excited as he spoke. "We can keep monitoring the rift, and make sure time-displaced animals are cared for before we send them back."

Down at the base of the stairs, Zoey raised a hand as she enjoyed Gladys and Georgie's company. "I volunteer as veterinary tribute."

"Done." Sebastian gazed over at his other operative. "How about you, Ev? There will be a need for Head of Security." He leaned his head toward Zoey. "Plus, since you and Beaumont have some weird *thing* go—"

"*Not* a thing," he retorted, then popped an ice cube in his mouth. "But I'm game."

After hearing everyone else chime in, Earnie sat forward and rubbed his knees. "Will any of these plans of yours cost me a pretty penny?"

Chuckling, Sebastian responded, "On the contrary, Mr. Pardy, I think you'll be quite happy with your compensation. And on top of that, you'll also be getting the best medical treatment SauraCorps can buy."

Earnie waved an indifferent hand. "Oh, I'm fine and fit as a fiddling frog. The nurse just said so hers—"

"You are the *heart and soul* of this place," Luz remarked, not wanting to experience another stroke scare. "We can't lose you, and...*I* need you."

"Well, now...." Taking her words to heart and giving everything a little more thought, Earnie finally nodded to himself. "Like my late Marilyn said, 'Every creature is a *gift*, and it's our *responsibility* to care for them.'" By the end of his sentence, he wore a proud smile. "Let's do it, Mr. Sharpe."

"Can my dad also work for you?" Luz inquired, drawing everyone's attention to her father while he gave her a surprised stare. "I just thought...it would be nice to have him even closer. Plus, he's pro at hauling dinosaurs around."

Embarrassed, Humberto rubbed the side of his face. "Doing it for the right reasons would definitely be less stressful."

"Why not make it a family affair?" Zav spread his arms wide, making himself a spectacle. "Does a SauraCorps outfit come with extra pairs of pants? I'm kinda going through those a fair bit lately."

Luz snorted. "He just needs diapers."

Sebastian squinted and tilted his head to the side at the odd request. "Uh, there's no outfits, sorry. But I'm sure I can make things work for both of you in some capacity." He returned to a more serious matter. "Plus, Humberto, if you have any more intel on El Cazador's cartel, my team would love to chat with you."

As the adults continued to figure out the details, Luz laid back in her reclining chair.

The gentle breeze brushed her hair against her cheek.

Animal vocalizations near and far brought her a sense of peace.

As sleepiness settled in, she whispered to herself, "We did it, *Mom.*"

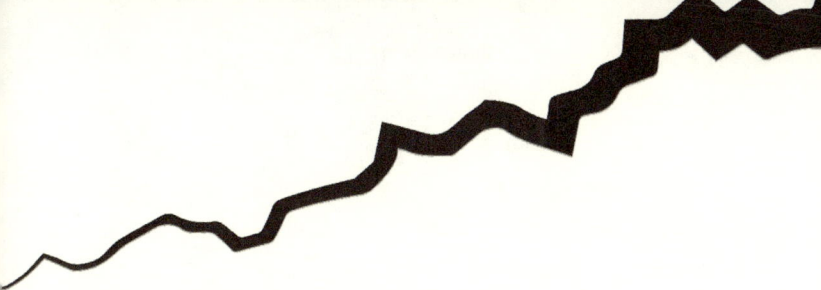

# END CREDITS SCENE

## ONE WEEK LATER

**OUT IN** a secluded area along one of Big Bend's rugged trails, Oliver Collins found a flat-top boulder and sat down. Checking his phone, he made sure to arrive early at the location he'd been given.

*Stay chill,* he thought, hyping himself up. *She'll take me back.*

He gazed around, taking in the brush and dark sky speckled with stars.

*SNAP!*

The sudden noise made him whip his gaze around. Spinning on the boulder, he made sure to check behind him.

"Hello, *Oliver.*"

Turning back, he strained his eyes to identify someone making their way toward him. "Daira? That you?"

Daira stood a few feet away and crossed her arms. "We need to talk."

"But...." He glanced around again. "Luz—*she* was the one who texted—"

"Oh, Luz, really?" Daira took another step. "But I thought you wanted *me*."

Gulping, Ollie locked eyes with her. "She, uh.... I mean, you're—"

"Ollie?" Luz stopped in her tracks, looking back and forth at them. "What are you doing here with *her?*"

Ollie thought about getting up and going to her, but something about the situation made him stay put. "Daira just showed up. I came here for you, Luz."

Tilting her head back and sighing, Daira shook her head. "Didn't you tell everyone at school that you and I were together?" She put a finger to her bottom lip. "I mean, you did try to kiss me."

He snorted. "Before you slapped me upside the head."

"You know it was well deserved."

"*Excuse me?*" Luz raised her voice. "Oliver Collins, you tried to *kiss her?*"

His legs locked up along with the rest of his body as he couldn't take both young women getting heated and irate. "But.... I-I-I, um.... I'm sorry, I tried to, but she—I didn't...."

Slow and ominous, Luz walked right up to Ollie.

She placed her hands on his shoulders.

Staring right into his eyes, she tensed her jaw. "Speak."

Taking a moment, Ollie took a deep inhale. "Lucero, I'm so—"

"Not you."

"Wh-what?"

"*Speak!*"

Utterly confused, Ollie hesitated before opening his mouth again.

Then he noticed her gazing past him, above his shoulder.

Something moved among the bushes and small trees behind him.

A reverberating growl pierced his entire being.

Getting off the boulder and taking small steps, he came face to face with large teeth.

The immense beast opened its mouth wide.

*RRRROOOOOOUUUUUUHH!*

Ollie immediately screamed.

Spinning back to the two girls, he shrieked again before taking off back to his car.

Daira busted a gut. "That…was *awesome!*" Pointing in Ollie's direction, she couldn't stop chuckling. "Pretty sure he wet his pants."

Luz grinned, placing an arm around Daira's shoulders and patting the dinosaur's snout. "We sure showed him, didn't we, Tess?"

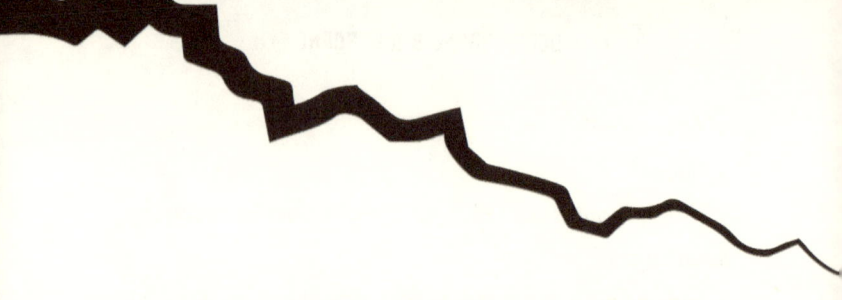

# EXTRA END CREDITS SCENE

## ONE YEAR LATER

**"THEY'RE ASKING** for it, Ev."

"*Ugh,* cameras." As Evander kept strolling down a red carpet in a crimson suit, he glanced over at the crowd of bothersome photographers. "*Double-ugh* for camera-people."

"Oh, come on!" By his side in a slimming black dress, Zoey slung her arm into his and pulled him back. "Just for a second."

"Fine." He rolled his eyes before making a half-grin.

Zo put on her best smile while striking a couple of poses. A barrage of flashes nearly blinded them.

Hands rested on each of their shoulders as someone brought their head between theirs.

"Have to say, you two might just be the *best-looking couple* here tonight."

They turned around to find Sebastian standing behind them.

"Hey, Seb!" Zo gave him a big hug. "Thanks for getting us tickets. This is so fancy."

Ev added, "Molly would've loved this, said she's sorry she couldn't get off work. They needed her for another surgery."

"I would've loved to finally meet her." Zo smirked. "You should give me her deets so I can invite her out for drinks… and tell funny stories about you."

He groan-chuckled. "Which is exactly why I haven't introduced you two yet."

"Wait…" Sebastian paused. "…so, you two never really—"

"We made great partners." Zo winked at Ev. "But not *partner* partners."

As the trio carried on down the walkway, Zo brought up, "Oh, by the way, Seb, we had a new arrival of a *velafrons* at the ranch yesterday. I'd never seen one before, I'll show you a picture—"

"Show me after." Sebastian hurried them along. "It's starting in less than fifteen minutes, and I need some popcorn."

Shuffling past others down an aisle, Sebastian popped a couple pieces of popcorn in his mouth. Moseying through a row, he finally claimed his reserved seat.

Noticing a certain young couple in front of him, he leaned forward. "Sorry, but…couldn't you have picked a better name than *Sterling?*"

Laughing out loud, Kamren Eckhardt turned around in his seat. "It fits the villain vibe so well, though."

"Sebastian!" Vivienne hopped out of her seat to give her friend a hug. "So good to see you. Is Felicia here?"

"Unfortunately, she couldn't make it," Sebastian answered as he sat back down. "But she wanted me to thank you for the earrings you made for her, Viv. You're *extremely* talented."

"Aw, thanks," she responded with a shy grin. "Is everything okay with her?"

He nodded. "She was having a bad nausea day, even though she's about six months along now."

"Oh, that's right!" Viv squealed in excitement. "Have you guys picked any names out?"

Kam smirked. "I can tell you right now, they'll be the *Sharpe*-est looking baby ever."

She smacked his shoulder. "You're running out of good material."

"Speaking of material…." Sebastian ate another morsel of popcorn. "How does it feel being at the world premiere of *Saura-Portal?*"

"This is…*so surreal,*" Kam remarked, taking it all in. "I've been so nervous about this that I haven't been able to write much of anything lately."

"That so?" Sebastian cleared his throat as he lowered his voice. "Well, I don't have all the details, but recent events could be spin-off-worthy."

Interested to hear more, Kamren turned in his seat. "Go on."

"Picture time-displaced dinosaurs on a ranch near Big Bend National Park in Texas…."

If you enjoyed your time on the ranch,
please take a moment to

# GIVE IT A REVIEW!

# MORE FROM DEREK BORNE

*IN CANONICAL ORDER:*

## THE ULTIMATE AGENT SERIES

*The Ultimate Agent* – Book 1
*The Helios Files* – UA Classified Anthology
*The Ultimate Agent* – Book 2
*The Ultimate Agent* – Book 3

## THE DINO-RIFT SERIES

*Dino-Rift*
*SauraCorps: Salvation* – A Dino-Rift Sequel

## SIDE NOTE:

There are subtle ties to the Ultimate Agent
series within the Dino-Rift books.

# COMING SOON

*Z-Z-ZAP! ZZZZEEEEUUUU-POP!*

Grass beneath Orva's knees altered to a hardened, greyish surface.

She no longer knelt among her village.

Her opposers had been whisked along with her.

Stepping back, the hostile Viking woman gazed around in a stupor.

Forest trees had been replaced with tall damaged structures with a smattering of broken windows throughout them.

A burly Viking pointed at the dark-haired woman before them. "*Witch!*"

Back on her feet, Orva scoffed. "You think *me* a witch?"

*Z-Z-ZAP! ZZZZEEEEUUUU-POP!*

Another swirl of incredible force exploded from behind her.

Orva shielded her eyes from the blinding effervescence with an armored arm. Once the whirlwind of oddity dissipated, her jaw shuddered as it dropped.

Taller than any man she'd ever seen, a massive feline with incisors half the length of her sword turned its head toward the small group. Waves of black stripes flowed down its light-brown, thick hide. Black spots decorated its robust, muscular legs. One of its legs had a strange blue fabric wrapped around it like a bandage of sorts.

A trepid Viking took aim with a crossbow he'd collected from a previous plunder.

*Thunk!*

*RROOOOOOAAAAAARRRR!*

Immediately, the overwhelmed feline reacted to the arrow lodged in its left hindleg.

Faster than any of them had anticipated, the monstrous cat bounded for them.

Whipping her shield up in time, Orva got knocked to the side by one of the animal's strong paws. Her backside hit the hard ground, sending a throbbing ache up her spine.

The Viking with the crossbow barely had any time to reload his weapon before his back crunched into a metallic shaft protruding from the ground. His agonizing scream got cut short as the feline sank its saber-teeth into him.

A simple jerk of the creature's head threw the man crashing into another Viking.

Bewildered by the entire turn of events, Orva watched in horror as the woman she'd clashed with made it only twenty feet away before getting slammed into the solid terrain from behind.

Growling, the feline flexed its claws into the woman's body, lowered its toothy maw, and finished her off.

*Good Lord.* Orva intensified the grip on her sword. *I have had enough of attacks for today.* Cautious, she got to her feet and withdrew by a couple of steps.

When she thought she had enough space between her and the giant cat, she spun around.

"*Halt, human.*" A figure with the stature of a human had an odd object attached to its right arm. "*You are not authorized to be in this zone.*"

The more it spoke to her, Orva found its tone sounded off. "I am...sorry?"

"*State your credentials,*" the figure demanded, powering up the object with a click. "*Name and registry digits.*"

"You do not understand, I have no idea of where I am," Orva threw back at the new individual. "If you could please—"

"*One moment.*" The odd figure replayed her voice from a source within itself.

Bringing a hand to her lips, anxiety seeped onto her face as she couldn't fathom how it had taken her voice and then emitted it as if it had become her. "How did you—"

"*Voice recognition: unidentifiable.*"

She held a hand up in defense. "My name is Orva, daughter of—"

"*Get down on the ground.*" The solid figure stepped forward with a seamless grace unlike any human. "*Place your hands behind your head. Interlace your fingers.*"

"Are you taking me captive?" Puzzled beyond belief, Orva retreated into an alley between two of the tall structures. "What is the meaning of this?" Upon a closer look, she noticed the figure had no skin. Only some kind of silver mask which glowed blue and red in parts.

With both of its hands now on the ominous object it had been carrying, it aimed right at her. "*Comply or be terminated.*"

"Beg your pardon?" Orva backed into a wall with nowhere left to go. Her hands tightened even more on her sword and shield. "Please, I do not mean any harm."

Identifying the weapon in the human's hand, a red light intensified in the middle of the figure's head. *"Threat confirmed. Notifying assista—"*

*Crunch!*

Dagger-like teeth forced their way through the individual's torso.

Orva didn't even blink as her unusual saviour chewed on the figure and swung it around like a child's doll. Unable to grasp the current happenings, she noticed small bits of lightning sparked out from the odd person's innards.

No blood. No guts.

Only small metallic strings of sorts spilled out from its body.

Orva failed to keep herself calm. *What on earth is going on?*

# ORVA

# ACKNOWLEDGEMENTS

**THERE'S A** reason why my wife's name is attached to the cover of this book. Not only is she my first eyes and ears on my projects, here's a little **Story Time:**

Back in 2023, I found myself in a creative burnout. Didn't want to write, my brain would constantly say "nope" whenever I opened a document.

But my wife was always there, encouraging and cheering me on. When 2024 hit, my brain finally let the floodgates fly open, and I found my mojo again. But when moments hit of struggling to find the right plot point (because I'm a pantser), my wife would always come in clutch with the perfect ideas.

A. L. Borne, you truly deserve this recognition and I never want to take my time with you for granted.

To my editor, Brooke, thank you so much for being a superfan of my work, and for caring about my stories and characters just as much as I do.

Molly Phipps, my cover designer and formatter @ We Got You Covered Book Design, just when I think you've outdone yourself, you've gone and taken my covers to the next level with EPICNESS.

To my Alpha and Beta readers, Jo, Amanda, Rebecca, and new additions Rosaly, Bailey, Marissa, and Victoria (my new dino author buddy), your help, support, and reassurance that the world needs my books continues to boost me whenever I'm doubting myself.

To my fellow authors and readers, you keep reminding me of why the book community is so amazing. When I thought these books with dinosaurs would never come of anything, you proved me wrong. The amount of love you and your kids show for the *Dino-Rift* series overwhelms me with pure joy.

Be someone's hero, don't take time for granted, and keep your family close.

**DEREK**

# ABOUT DEREK BORNE

**DEREK BORNE** is a Canadian author who lives in "the prettiest town in Ontario" with his wife and Libby, their drama queen kitty. Always telling stories since a young age, he first wrote The Ultimate Agent at fourteen, and kept writing as a hobby over the years until finally publishing in 2017. When he isn't writing, he's selling olive oil and balsamic vinegars, watching hockey, and waiting for the next superhero and dinosaur movie to come out. And most likely eating pizza.

Find out more at **derekborne.weebly.com**.

www.ingramcontent.com/pod-product-compliance
Lightning Source LLC
Chambersburg PA
CBHW020648030726
47498CB00002B/417